Typhoon

Savage Brotherhood MC: Book Five

A Paranormal Romance

by Jasmine Wylder

Chapter One

Mia

Blood spurted across her face. Mia snarled under her breath. She pinched an artery shut with a clamp as her tiger paced and growled in her chest. If she had an extra set of hands to help...but the shifters who came in after the attack were all fucking useless, and the help she'd hired two months before had quit on her after one of the geniuses groped her in the clinic.

Even though she'd torn the offender a new one, it wasn't going to bring her nurse back.

Mia shoved the thoughts from her head, as she grabbed a sterile needle with thread and moved quickly to sew the torn flesh together. The good thing about doctoring shifters was that they healed quickly. As long as she got this put back together, her patient would live. She swallowed hard, blinking sweat from her eyes as she connected the pieces that needed to be connected. She suctioned out the blood, and no new blood oozed in. Good—it meant the man was already healing.

She didn't let herself slow until the gaping wound had been closed. Only then did she take a moment to breathe before cleaning up the wound, checking to make sure her patient was still out of it, and tossing all of her instruments into a solution of rubbing alcohol. She stripped off her blood-stained gloves and smock and scrubbed down. Exhaustion ached in her bones, but this was the worst of the men brought in.

She opened the door and pointed at a couple of burly men who had showered as she'd instructed them to do earlier. “You two: come help me get him into another room.”

They both scowled at her order, but her fierce glare cut off any arguments they might have had. They did as she asked, and soon the shifter on which she'd been operating was in a private room, hooked to machines to monitor his vitals. A slim, blond woman with the faint odor of fox about her sat beside his bed.

Mia didn't wonder if she'd done a good enough job. She didn't have time when there were others in need of her care. The vampire attack had been vicious. Fortunately, there had been no bites. Even though the shifters had recently learned how to keep from going rabid after a bitten by a vampire, the best medicine was not to get bitten at all.

Two of the men had bad gashes on their arms and legs that Mia had to stitch up, but nothing as bad as the first one. She had those men lie down in another room while she checked over the others to make sure they had no internal injuries.

"Hey, Doc," one of the men grunted as he got to his feet. Blood dribbled down his chest. "What about me?"

"What about you?" Mia snapped at him. "You're fine. Sit down and rest."

"Nah, I need some...help." He winked at her as he slid forward. The wolf stink clung strongly to him. "Something to get the blood pumping and healing, you know?"

Mia rolled her eyes, pinning him with a fierce glare. She could actually feel her irises change color from a dull amber-brown to vivid gold. Her tiger pressed against the surface, wishing for release. She was a solitary cat. All the canines in her clinic had the effect of driving her good sense away.

"Care to say that again?" she asked coolly, keeping her voice low. "Or would you prefer I rip your balls off and feed them to you now?"

The wolf's eyes widened slightly before he dropped to a fighting stance. Before he could say another word, half a dozen of the others had jumped to their feet and put themselves between Mia and the wolf. A loud growl rippled through the air, and they all cringed. Mia felt a strong reaction to the growl herself, her tiger having recognized the presence of an alpha.

While the others responded by ducking their heads and deferring to the strength shown, Mia's tiger purred, and heat twisted inside of her. The exhaustion seemed to lift as a thrill of excitement surged through her blood; she would recognize Typhoon's growl anywhere.

The shifters parted to reveal Typhoon standing behind the wolf that had propositioned Mia. His dark eyes had narrowed, and his jaw was clenched. He glanced around at the members. As alpha of the Savage Brotherhood, a motorcycle club—some would call it a gang—that protected unknowing civilians from vampires, he was an impressive sight. Taller than any of the others, his shoulders were almost too broad to fit through a regular door. Muscles strained against his shirt. Mia had told him once that his body deserved to be in a calendar for July and August.

His response? “I know.” He'd said it with a wink that set Mia’s heart to fluttering followed by a night that would not be forgotten.

Now, there was nothing flirtatious about Typhoon’s expression. Fury radiated off him in waves that had Mia’s tiger hissing. She backed away as Typhoon strode through the crowd to gaze at a short, muscular coyote.

“How many dead?” Typhoon snarled.

The coyote lifted his chin. In some, it would seem a belligerent move, but with canids, it was a show of submission. “None on our side. The vamps were in our territory, I—”

"Took unnecessary risks!" Typhoon bellowed. His hand lashed out to seize the coyote by the scruff. "I have had it up to here with you putting men in danger with your stupid schemes. If anybody had died, your head would be on the wall right now."

Mia strode forward. She shoved Typhoon in the chest and drew herself up. Even though she was a good head shorter than him—he was huge, even for a wolf—she didn't let him intimidate her. "Not in my clinic."

Typhoon snarled. Mia bunched her hands on her hips and widened her stance. "Get out until you can calm down and act reasonably."

"You think I'm going to take orders from—"

"From the doctor whom you rely upon to patch up your men? Yes." Mia stepped closer and narrowed her eyes. "Get out now, or I shall have to put these boys in a position where their loyalty is tested between the two of us."

Typhoon didn't look at the murmuring shifters to see them bounce from one foot to the other. It really wasn't fair to put them in this position, but if he didn't leave, she would tell them to take Typhoon out. He was alpha, and they'd obey him in anything...but she was their doctor, and for many of them, the only person they really trusted.

She was confident they would side with her if worse came to worst. At least, most of them would.

Luckily, it didn't come to that. Typhoon snorted, shook his head, and stepped past her. “I want to see who was injured. I can smell their blood. Someone was hurt badly.”

Mia nodded and fell into step beside him. “This way. He'll be all right. There’s a little otter-shifter who was very badly hurt, but he’s going to make a full recovery with enough rest.”

“Good.” Typhoon put a hand on her shoulder as soon as the others were out of sight. “What would I do without you?”

Mia snorted. “Die, probably.”

Typhoon let out a rare, low chuckle. “You’re probably right, there. Thank you, Mia.”

She didn’t respond to that. It wouldn't be much longer before he'd have to make do without her. This wasn’t going to be her life forever, especially not with Jasper waiting for her back home. Her little boy was the world to her. She never got a moment's rest with her job, and she was constantly having to leave him to the care of others. No, she had to have something less…erratic. For his sake.

As she showed Typhoon to the otter's room, Mia's stomach curled in on itself. She snuck a glance at Typhoon from the corner of her eye. That one wild night they'd spent together had ended with Jasper in her arms nine months later. Typhoon knew she'd had a baby. He also knew the timing was right, but he never asked, and Mia wasn’t about to tell him.

Typhoon was the alpha of the largest organization of shifters. He was always on guard against the threat of vampires who consistently tried to take more than their share. What did a man like that want with a baby in his life?

***

The babysitter was sleeping on the couch when Mia got home. She was curled up with a pillow under her head and a textbook on her chest. Mia flinched. It was bad enough to be called away in the middle of the night, but poor Gracie had exams coming up. It wasn't fair to call her in on such short notice all the time. Mia had a list of babysitters, but it was the same story with all of them.

Jasper started fussing from his bedroom, as though he could sense her presence. Mia shrugged off her coat, hung it up, and brushed her damp hair away from her face. She'd showered before leaving the clinic, leaving instructions for the boys staying to watch after their brothers and call her if there was any change or if they had any worries. The scent of blood was no longer on her skin, at least.

Jasper's cries became more insistent, and she hurried to him, hoping Gracie would stay asleep. Jasper lifted his head and grinned at her as soon as she stepped into his bedroom. At four months, he was still a little small for his age but more developed more in other areas. He was already recognizing his own face in the mirror and preferred her company over strangers.

"Hey there, sunshine." She lifted him out of the crib as he struggled to push himself to his hands and knees. Mia tenderly stroked his downy-soft hair and kissed his forehead. Though she knew getting him down again later would be a bit of a challenge, she didn't want to waste any time she had with him. "How is Mommy's little man doing?"

Jasper put his hands on either side of her face and spat a raspberry at her. Mia jerked back, laughing. It was just what she needed after the hard day she'd had. She cradled her son in her arms, smiling at him. Her smile slipped a little when she remembered his father at the clinic earlier in the day.

Typhoon was the kind of guy that never went with the same girl twice. Mia knew that. She'd seen it multiple times. If someone took his fancy, he was charming without making what he wanted a secret. His voice got deep and gravelly, and his eyes glowed with anticipation. There weren’t many girls who could say no to a guy like that. Mia had done her best, keeping her distance and playing it cool, challenging his authority every chance she got, trying to turn his attentions elsewhere.

It hadn’t worked. That one night she'd spent with him? It was nothing like she'd expected. It was powerful. It was explosive. But it had also been gentle. He'd treated her like a queen as he'd claimed her. There were times she'd wanted to phone him up and try it again, but that wasn’t going to happen. She was on birth control, and they'd used a condom when she'd gotten pregnant with Jasper, which was testament as to Typhoon's virility. She wasn’t going to risk getting pregnant again, especially not with a four-month-old baby. Not to mention, Typhoon would probably laugh at her—she was nothing more than the girl for whom he'd had an itch, and that itch had been scratched.

As she bounced Jasper, earning giggles from him, her phone rang. Mia's heart dropped; there was only one reason she'd get a call then. She pulled her phone from her pocket to see it wasn't the clinic calling. Nor was it any of her other contacts in the Savage Brotherhood. At least, not that she had for work.

It was Blake, another wolf shifter, the disgraced alpha of the Cherryvale chapter. He and Typhoon were bitter rivals in the gang, but he was also one of the only people who could give her what she wanted.

If he only had better hours...

"What do you want?" she snapped at him, pinching the phone between her shoulder and ear as she took Jasper to her room. Gracie had already planned to stay there overnight. If she woke up on her own, Mia would send her home.

"Just checking up on you. Making sure that my grand prize is taking care of herself."

Mia's nostrils flared. She hated the way he talked about her, but it was true enough. Blake ran an auction, catering to the Brotherhood. He sold anything and everything they wanted, up to and including mates. The clientele coming to his auctions were rich. The door cover at his swanky club ensured it.

It hadn't been an easy decision, choosing to auction herself off to be married to somebody in the gang—who knew who'd end up buying her? But Mia was tired. She was tired of being woken up in the middle of the night to sew up bloody, sliced-up guts. She was tired of being alone every night when she went to bed. She was just tired of it all. Yeah, maybe selling herself into marriage wasn't the most logical choice, but with her life, she didn't have time to meet, date, and fall in love. It didn't matter. As long as the man buying her wasn't abusive, she had the need for neither love nor fidelity.

She wanted stability. She wanted safety. She wanted to be sure vampires wouldn't come after her and her son because they knew that without their doctor, the Brotherhood would be severely crippled. She didn't want Jasper to be involved in any of it.

“I’m fine,” Mia murmured, letting her voice growl. “Or I would be if you didn't check up on me. I’m not your property. If you keep acting like this, I’m going to pull out of the auction.”

Blake was silent for a moment. “I heard you had a tough time after an attack. Are you okay?”

Mia sighed. It was times like that she thought he might actually be genuine. “Yeah, I’m fine. Just tired. Stop calling me. I’ll be at the auction tomorrow night, don’t worry.”

Unless she was called into work. Then again, they had a video for just that occasion. Either that or Blake would simply reschedule her auction. It really didn’t really matter; it was happening—it didn't matter when.

She hung up the phone and cradled Jasper against her chest. He immediately started to root around, looking to feed, and Mia unbuttoned her blouse. She looked at her little boy, remembering why she was doing this.

Life as a single working mom wasn't for her. She needed a partner. The man who would buy her would know she had a son; it would mean he wanted a child in his life. She let out a sigh as she sank into the bed and got comfortable. It would work out. Somehow, it would work out.

Chapter Two

Typhoon

The smell of combined exhaust and blood had been exhilarating. Typhoon had licked his lips, enjoying the sensation of wind blowing against his face. After Reynolds' disastrous attempt to clear out a coven of vampires camping on Brotherhood territory yesterday, that today's mission would go smoothly was the best he could have hoped for. Typhoon had stayed out of it, observing how Twister, a young wolf who had just applied for the position of alpha of the Cherryvale chapter, behaved and how well he led. For the most part, Twister was qualified.

They pulled into the warehouse where they'd stash the loot from the job they were about to pull. Typhoon wasn't overly fond of jobs robbing civilians, but they had to be done. Running the Brotherhood wasn't cheap, after all, and he wasn't going to rely on people like Hurricane for handouts. The bastards they were about to rob were already too rich to spend it all in one lifetime, besides. What did it matter if they were a couple thousand poorer? It was a redistribution of resources, nothing more.

"All right, men," Twister said as they dismounted their bikes, "go get some food and water, and then we can go over everything you did wrong."

Typhoon rolled his eyes as he removed the bag of money he'd stashed in his bike.

Twister glanced at him and grimaced. "First, though, we count up what we collected and put it in the safe." That was the biggest problem when it came to Twister. He was dynamic, charismatic, and commanded attention. His men liked him and obeyed his orders, but it was a relatively small group—only thirty of them—and he could get away with treating them individually. Playing mother hen at times instilled loyalty in the men because they wanted someone to look out for them. It would be very different dealing with a full city. He wouldn't get to know each member of the chapter and would have to be far stricter. Challenges would be common. The way Twister handled things, the men would think him tenderhearted—which he was.

The question was: did he have the balls to get bloody when it was necessary?

Twister's men hurried to obey him, laying out what they'd collected before getting food and water. Twister counted up the money, listed the jewelry they'd taken, and locked it all in the safe.

Typhoon lounged on a couch set on a secondary platform in the warehouse as the men went over the events of the day. He knew they were nervous to have him there, as they should be. Typhoon also had the feeling they were far more eager to obey Twister promptly; they wanted him to succeed.

Typhoon yawned as he listened with half an ear. It didn't matter if they wanted him to succeed or not. In the end, Twister just wasn't cut out to be alpha at that time. It was something he told Twister as soon as his men had been dismissed. Disappointment hit the smaller wolf's face hard, though he nodded his acceptance.

"Mind telling me what I need to do to improve?" Twister asked him. "We can talk about it over dinner. I have an invite to The Bombshell."

Typhoon almost snarled, but he wasn't about to make a habit of waving his rivalry with Hailstorm, The Bombshell's proprietor, around. He clicked his teeth together and nodded. "As long as you're paying."

"Of course," Twister replied promptly. "It's the least I can do to repay you."

Typhoon shook his head as he got back on his bike. That was another thing that Twister had against him: he was too honorable. You did him a favor, and he wanted to pay the favor back. It didn't matter how small the favor was, he wanted to show his appreciation. Sometimes—many times—Typhoon even wondered why he was with the Brotherhood at all.

He knew, of course. Typhoon made a habit out of knowing the names and histories of the new recruits. Twister had as much reason as anybody to hate vampires. He wasn't in it for the money and excitement—he was in it to protect civilians. Twister was naïve to think most of the others had joined for the same reason, though.

They made it to The Bombshell quickly. At the sight of Typhoon, the bouncer let them in without asking for an invite. Typhoon had expected it, just as he'd expected Hailstorm to greet him personally no more than half a minute later.

There was a certain glee in the other wolf's eye, a pleased look on his face. "Typhoon, I never expected you to one day grace my humble little establishment."

"Hailstorm," Typhoon greeted, "I'm here because the kid wants to talk business, nothing more."

Twister's face tinged pink. "I've been looking forward to seeing what your auctions are like for a long time."

Hailstorm's gaze didn't leave Typhoon's face. His smile was wide, his white teeth gleaming. "Well, you're in luck. We've got a good lineup tonight. If there's anything I can do for you, please let me know. I'll have Gerome get you a good seat."

Typhoon had been curious about Hailstorm's place, he had to admit. As he and Twister were led to a table close to a large, highly polished stage, Typhoon glanced around. Hailstorm had clearly done well by himself with the joint. The carpets were a forest green with golden-brown trim. The walls had been painted to match. Crystal chandeliers hung from the ceiling. Each table was adorned with a unique, glowing centerpiece. From the smells curling into his nostrils, the food also promised to be amazing.

A bottle of fancy wine arrived at the table, compliments of the house.

Twister smiled as he ordered a plate of lobster and crab. “I should take you on dates more often,” he laughed, and then his face turned white. “I mean...I didn’t mean...It was a joke. I’m not into guys.”

Typhoon snorted, relaxing a little as he ordered a large plate of spaghetti and meatballs, extra meatballs. “Don’t worry about it.”

Twister nodded, but he didn’t relax. Typhoon didn’t see a reason to beat about the bush, so he clasped his hands and leaned on the table with his elbows. “You aren’t alpha material, Twister. I know that’s disappointing for you, but you’d have to make some serious changes before you'd be considered for a position.”

“I’m willing to make changes.”

“Are you really? As alpha, you'd have to present a strong front at all times. Your men can’t question you, and you can’t be their friend. You’re far better suited to smaller groups, like the one you have, where you know each of them individually and can adjust your dealings with them on an individual basis. You can't do that as alpha of a chapter. You have to be tough. You have to be willing to make them bleed if they won't listen to you."

Twister leaned back in his chair. He frowned, mulling it over. "I don't think that's the only way."

Typhoon snorted. "I've been alpha of the Savage Brotherhood for thirteen years now, Twister. I didn't get this position by being kind-hearted."

"But you don't come down on your subordinates without any mercy at all," Twister argued. "I mean, look at Tornado in Coalfell and Thunder in Ivywood...hell, even Hurricane—they all stepped out of line, and you didn't give them—"

“They corrected their mistakes,” Typhoon interrupted, snarling as he glared at Twister. “And that is far different from the men who'll stab you in the back the moment they decide they want to be alpha instead of you.”

Now, it was Twister’s turn to lean on the table. His expression was intense. “My recruiter told me I’d never among to anything in the Brotherhood because I wasn’t willing to have unnecessary casualties when dealing with civilians. I told him that I was going to make it, and I wasn’t going to sacrifice my morals for it. I believe our brothers are far more interested in doing the right thing than you give them credit for.”

“*And* you’re a dreamer.”

Typhoon shook his head. He remembered when he used to be a

dreamer. That was when he'd also thought that love was enough to change the impossible, before his mother died, and before he learned the truth of the world. He envied Twister in some ways: he was still able to dream, even after the pain he'd been through.

"I just think that you can attract more flies with honey than vinegar."

"Which is all well and good if you're looking to set a trap, but this—" He cut off as Hailstorm strutted onto the stage. "We can finish this conversation after Hailstorm finishes his blathering." Typhoon snorted and poured himself a glass of wine. "Anybody who buys a mate at auction must be truly desperate."

"I don't know. I think most of them just want someone to hold when they get home," Twister mused.

"That's what brothels are for."

Twister gave him an incredulous look, but he didn't comment. Their meals came, and Typhoon eagerly heaped a quarter pound of cheese on top of his spaghetti before mixing it all together with the sauce. He caught Hailstorm glancing at him as the first person in the auction came onstage. Sex trafficking was one of the few illegal pursuits in which Typhoon forbade the gang from participating. However, when the people on sale were of-age and willing, he had no issue with it.

The first two were men, both groomed impeccably with bodies that spoke to how they had taken care of themselves while not appearing overly muscular and dominating. Typhoon had to admit there was an appeal to that.

The next woman had the perfect porn-body: small waist, large breasts, narrow, curvy hips, and a tight ass. She giggled as she twirled around, and Typhoon admired her long, lean legs. Now, those would be something to lay between.

The fourth person was also a woman. When he saw her, Typhoon choked on a mouthful of noodles. He coughed violently and grabbed a napkin with which he covered his mouth. Twister asked him if he was okay, but Typhoon waved him off.

Once his airways were clear, he drained his wine and wiped his mouth with the back of his hand.

His coughing had drawn Mia's attention, but she deliberately ignored him as she smiled at the crowd. She was wearing a shimmering gold-and-black dress that imitated the stripes on her tiger's body. There was a thin strap on one side holding up the top, which molded to her large breasts. The slit stopped mid-thigh, showing off every curve of her body. She even wore sparkling black heels, which had to be at least five inches high.

Typhoon's hands clenched the table.

She'd been warning him that she was going to quit working for the gang for some time, but he hadn't believed she was serious. And now, this?

"Many of you already know me," she said. She smiled without any of the vapid giggling of the last woman. “I’m Mia Efron, tiger shifter and mother to a four-month-old son, Jasper. I’ve worked for many, many years as a doctor, and I want to have a break.” She jutted out a hip, put her hand on it, and winked. “And a little fun. Want a sugar baby? I’m your gal.”

There was something about the way she'd said it that drove Typhoon to his feet. If she wanted to retire, fine, but why come to Hailstorm’s sleazy club to auction herself off like that? “What the fuck do you think you're doing?”

Hailstorm and Mia both jumped. She turned to him and said, “I just said what I’m doing. Looking for a sugar daddy. I told you I’m quitting the practice.”

"And you decided that you wanted to marry some jerk with enough money to see women as a commodity?"

Mia shrugged. "What's it to you?"

Typhoon slammed his fist into the table, and he sat back down, nostrils flaring. It wasn't like he cared what she did, but getting involved with Hailstorm? Clearly, he'd been mistaken when he'd thought she had even one lick of good sense.

"You can always bid for her, you know."

Typhoon snarled as he turned on Twister, who flinched but met his gaze, nevertheless. "If you're that upset about somebody else buying her, *you* can buy her instead. Hailstorm's got a policy that if both parties aren't satisfied with their marriages after a month then they're annulled, and the money's returned to the buyer."

"Why would I want to marry her?" Typhoon growled. He gestured for the waiter, his appetite suddenly gone.

Twister grimaced a moment and then shrugged. "You just seemed concerned, is all. Actually, I'm going to call Roxy to see if she'll lend me some money. I don't see Mia getting into something like this willingly."

The auction had started to wind down. Twister wasn't going to get his money in time.

Mia smiled at the highest bidder thus far, an older musk-ox shifter whose leer told Typhoon all he needed to know about him. What was she thinking, exposing her son to all of this?

"And the bid is closing at—"

Typhoon leaped to his feet with a roar, cutting Hailstorm off.

Everything went silent as the entire club stopped to stare at him.

Mia's eyes were wide, uncharacteristically startled.

Typhoon clenched his fists and jumped onto the stage.

Hailstorm backed away a step as he approached, but Typhoon's gaze was on Mia alone.

"How much was the last bid?" he demanded.

"Twenty-five thousand."

"Make it twenty-six." Typhoon turned his glower onto Hailstorm. "And she's going home with me."

Hailstorm gaped at him, a stupid expression on his face.

The back of Typhoon's neck prickled when he realized everybody was staring at him, wearing the same expression. They were wondering what he was doing, what secret feelings he might harbor for the curvy tiger. His jaw tightened. She was his doctor. That was all. If she was really going to leave him in the lurch, he wanted every detail as to why.

"Twenty-six, it is," Hailstorm stuttered. "We can discuss payment options later. If you'll take your new mate through there," he gestured to a door, "you'll be married right away."

Typhoon scowled, but he took Mia's arm and pulled her toward the door. He'd find out what it was all about and send her back. In the meantime, they’d be married, all right.

She stared at him, still gaping and looking uncertain.

Good. Maybe it meant she'd be more cooperative when he tried to get answers out of her.

Chapter Three

Mia

Mia stared at Typhoon's profile as the bored-looking wedding officiate rattled out the necessities of the marriage. It had to be a dream. Out of everyone she knew and everyone who had been at the auction, he was the last person she'd expected to bid on her, let alone shell out twenty-six thousand dollars. That was a hell of a lot of money; it was a quarter of what she earned in a year. True, she could have jobs that paid more...but still, it was a lot to pay out for her.

Was it because he'd wanted her to stay on at the clinic for him? She'd been telling him she was going to quit for months now!

Hot anger welled in her chest. Her hands clenched. If he wasn't genuine about this...Considering how angry he was, there was something more than just the auction on his mind.

Her nostrils flared as the officiate finished and they signed the paper legalizing their marriage. A couple of witnesses signed as well, and then it was done.

"Come on," Typhoon grunted at her, a heavy scowl on his face.

"Being your sugar baby doesn't mean I'm your slave," she told him flatly. She folded her arms over her chest and glared at him.

"Did I say you were a slave?" Typhoon glared at her. "I am well aware that you aren't going to obey my every word, but I have a plate of food that is getting cold, and we need to talk. So, let's go back to the dining room before the next 'couple' comes through."

The derision in his voice was more than enough to tell her what he thought of the whole business. Mia grunted as she stomped after him. Why had she worn heels? The pair she'd chosen was impossible to walk in, though they made her legs and butt look terrific. Still, if it was just for Typhoon, it hardly seemed worth the effort.

"I didn't know you had that kind of money," she hissed at him, her tiger pacing in her chest.

"Well, I do." He glanced back at her and slowed his long strides so she could keep up. They exited the little room and were ushered back to the dining hall.

Blake was introducing a pair of women who caressed each other as they gazed over the crowd. The old bidder—the one who had nearly gotten her—jumped out of his seat in his excitement to get to the women. Mia sat at the table with Typhoon and Andy Franks—who was well-known around the clinic (mostly for looking after other people)—with her elbows resting on the table. She didn't care if the posture wasn't ladylike.

"I'm not continuing on as a doctor at your clinic," Mia said, narrowing her eyes at Typhoon. "So, if you think you can bully me into staying, you have another thing coming. I have to have a different life. For my son's sake."

"Your son?" he repeated, narrowing his eyes.

Goddesses help her. Normally, Mia wasn't a religious woman, but every once in a while, she found herself pleading to various healer-goddesses for their aid. This time, she wasn't certain they'd help if they existed. She glared at Typhoon as he stuffed his face with pasta, which looked and smelled delicious.

Her mouth watered at the sight of Andy's lobster and crab, too. Andy silently passed a slice of toast over to her.

"Thanks," she murmured. She took a bite to steady herself before turning back to Typhoon. "I have a son. You've *met* Jasper before. Remember last week when you came in with that bear with a knife in his gut? Did you think I'd just picked up a random baby to bring to my clinic for an emergency case?"

"I know you have a son. What were you thinking, signing up for something like this? You had no idea who was going to buy you...do you think he," Typhoon pointed at the older man, who had just bought the right to marry the two young women, "would have been a good father?"

Andy bent over his dish and ate rapidly.

Mia glanced at him. Her gaze brought Typhoon's gaze to him as well.

Andy jumped to his feet. "I'm going to get the check."

"You do that." Typhoon cursed under his breath and shoved his half-eaten plate toward her. "Eat. I can hear your stomach from here. I can't believe this. It's a fine mess you've gotten me into."

Mia protested as she ate half a meatball.

"You never said anything about wanting to do something like this. With a child, I thought...well, I wanted to make sure." Typhoon glanced around the room. A slight pinkness came to his ears. "People are going to think I'm soft on you. All of my best men have been getting soft on women, and I'm not about to join them. They've all been acting like idiots." He leaned back, scowling as he folded his massive arms. His tattoos, always bold and black against his skin, seemed to pop out even more than his muscle. "I don't know what's happening with the Brotherhood these days. Damn wolves are getting whipped by a bunch of cats."

Mia had been eating as rapidly as she could, partly to give herself time to avoid saying something she'd regret and partly because she needed something in her stomach. She'd been so nervous that day, she hadn't really eaten anything. Typhoon's words, however, made her nostrils flare.

"Well, you like *my* cat well enough," she snapped at him.

Typhoon glanced at her. For a moment, she thought he was going to smile, but then his scowl darkened. "That is hardly the same thing. Looking for a night of fun doesn't get somebody tied down and acting like an idiot."

“Acting like an idiot: like dropping twenty-six thousand dollars on some pussy?”

“Oh, is that what you are?” Typhoon took his plate back. “And here I thought I was being a gentleman, making sure you weren’t being sold against your will.”

Before Mia could respond, Blake was suddenly at their table and Andy behind him. A broad smile crossed Blake’s face as his eyes latched onto Typhoon. “Is there a problem, My Alpha?”

If she wouldn't have looked like a jerk saying it, Mia would have said yes and broken the whole arrangement, but the last few days of him constantly checking up on her and the way he was almost gloating now, she couldn't help it.

"Nothing's wrong, no," she snapped, "except that this pasta has far too much salt in it."

Hailstorm opened his mouth, closed it, and forced another smile. "I'm sorry to hear that. It's on the house. I can go get a replacement—"

"No." Typhoon stood and threw a handful of bills on the table. "The spaghetti was fine. We don't have a problem here, I'll take this to go, along with the rest of the lobster there."

Andy glanced warily at him and reached for his own wallet, but a half-glare from Typhoon froze him in place. Hailstorm stood awkwardly for a moment, as though he were weighing his options, and then he shook his head. "Of course. I'll have this boxed for you, right away."

He took the plates and stalked away, probably cursing Typhoon for making such a scene in his club, when he had no choice but to act graciously. The old man and two girls came from the wedding room, all of them laughing and beaming at each other. Typhoon glared at them, making them skirt the table nervously.

Andy bounced on his toes and cleared his throat. "So, I'll pay for dinner another time," he said, keeping his voice low.

Typhoon opened his mouth. He grunted, then nodded.

Soon, they were on their way. Mia had taken the bus there, so she climbed onto the back of Typhoon's bike—her skirt hiking up to her hips, so her lace underwear pressed against Typhoon's jeans—and they were off. The wind blew in her hair, helping to calm her tiger's growling. It was clear the conversation wasn't over.

They stopped by her place first. Typhoon's phone rang as soon as they came to a stop. "Go on inside," Typhoon told her, gazing at his phone with a dark look on his face. "I'll take care of this."

Mia shrugged and went inside. Gracie was at the kitchen table, a plate of uneaten food beside her as she poured over her textbooks.

"Baby asleep?"

Gracie jumped. "Oh! I didn't hear you come in. Yeah, he went down about half an hour ago. Did you have fun on your date?"

Mia scowled. "It's complicated. I think he's coming in so we can talk, so you'd better go home."

"Are...are you sure?" Gracie's face fell into a frown. "Are you all right?"

"Yeah, I'm fine. It's just a complicated situation. I'm fine, I promise." Mia patted her shoulder and smiled reassuringly. "Go on home. I'll call you in an hour if you're worried."

Gracie didn't look completely reassured, but she nodded before gathering up her books and leaving. Mia saw her out and then waited in the doorway for Typhoon, who seemed distinctly agitated as he crammed his phone into his pocket. He gripped the handles of his bike, and Mia made a choking sound—he wasn't going to take off, was he?

“Business?” she asked quickly to remind him she was still there.

“Yeah,” he grunted before stalking into the house.

He let out a deep breath as she closed the door behind them. Typhoon peered back at Mia with a strange look in his eyes. He let his gaze roam down her figure. The look sent an excited shiver zinging straight to her core, even as Mia pulled in a deep breath to tell him she hadn't forgotten about their earlier conversation.

Typhoon stripped off his leather jacket, his hungry gaze roaming all over her. “So, what exactly does a sugar baby do for her sugar daddy?”

“Uh…well, you know…it’s a marriage. It depends on the individual contracts.” Why had her mouth gotten so dry? She swallowed and moved past him to clean up a little in the kitchen. “Basically, I’m your girlfriend and wife when you need me to be, and in exchange, you give me money and presents.”

“What does someone like you need a sugar daddy for? You could be earning twice as much money as you are now...under different circumstances.”

Mia shrugged. Her heart pattered against her ribs as if it wanted to burst out. She thought about pulling him down to her lips, but her tiger growled, as irritated at her sudden mood switch as she was. “I want the space to do the things I won't have time for if I’m working, like taking my son to parks and things, being home with him, going shopping without worrying about always having my phone on me because I might get called in."

Typhoon's huge, hot hands clamped around her waist, and he spun her around without warning and pressed her against the wall. His dark eyes burned with increased hunger as he leaned in closer. "So, did you expect your own credit cards or would you rather have a salary?"

Mia was unable to respond for several moments. Her brain nearly short-circuited. Was this really Typhoon, the same guy who never had a girl more than once? The all-powerful alpha who never took no for an answer?

"A salary would be fine," she managed. "Monthly or bi-weekly?"

Typhoon's hand traced the curve of her hip as he pondered. "Bi-weekly. How does three-thousand sound?"

Three-thousand every two weeks; six-thousand a month. It was two-thousand more than she'd been earning, which was pretty intense. She let out a shaky breath and nodded. It would be plenty to get by on. Where would Typhoon get that kind of money? Did he plan to pay her from Brotherhood funds, or was he secretly rich?

"It sounds good."

Typhoon grinned as he brushed the hair away from her neck. "Then pour some sugar on me."

Zings of pleasure went through her. His teeth grazed her neck, curling her core. She wrapped her arms around his neck. The argument concerning the clinic seemed far away as she dug her fingers into his hair and undulated her hips as they pressed against him.

Typhoon lifted her dress and hooking his thumbs beneath her underwear.

As he stroked her through the lace, a loud squawk-squeal rang through the house. They jumped and drew back from each other. Typhoon turned his face toward the kitchen door, frowning heavily. “Is that—”

“My son, yes.” She pushed against his chest and shook her head. “I have to go take care of him. When he’s like this, he won’t calm down on his own.”

The cry again, louder this time.

Typhoon snorted, and he stepped back. “That's going to get tiresome. Are you sure that—”

“You married me knowing I had a son,” Mia snapped. It was *his* son. Surely he'd wondered, given the timing of his birth. They were careful, but it wasn't like it was one-hundred percent effective. He had to have wondered. “If you don’t like the fact that my baby’s needs take precedence over your wants, then you can just go back to Blake and tell him to annul the arrangement.”

Typhon scowled. “I don’t intend to go back to him for anything.”

“Then you’ll have to deal with the fact that I’m a mother. We don’t have to live together.” Jasper let out another, louder cry, then he grew quiet. “I have to go.”

"But he's quiet now."

"He's listening for me. If I don't go, he'll get really mad."

Mia strode from the kitchen, chewing her lip as she walked, trying to keep it together.

Typhoon followed after her, but before they got too far, his phone rang again.

Mia hesitated for a moment before disappearing into Jasper's room. He'd pulled himself to his knees and was leaning against the side of the crib in an awkward position. "Come here, baby."

She pulled her baby into her arms and glanced at the hallway where she could hear Typhoon talking on his phone. Mia crept to the door and peered out.

Typhoon's expression was furious as he clutched his phone. "I told you never to phone me," Typhoon snarled. "Now twice, in one night? No, I don't want to see you. No—" He looked up suddenly, as though he'd just realized that Mia was watching, and let out a snarl that made Jasper whimper.

Mia's tiger growled back.

Typhoon turned on his heel and headed for the door. "Fine. I'm coming to see you." He hung up as he stormed out the door, slamming it behind him.

Chapter Four

Typhoon

It was the last thing he wanted to deal with at that moment.

He'd intended to leave Mia at her house and pick up their conversation in the morning when he'd be less agitated. Then he'd gotten the first call, and he needed a distraction to calm down. And then there was the second call. He knew if he stayed, Mia would ask him what it was all about. The mood had already been broken, so there wasn't any point in sticking around.

Typhoon jumped onto his bike and rode hard to meet the man who called him. The man—whom he never wanted to lay eyes on again—was the man who had haunted his nightmares for years.

There was a small logging road that led to an open area a half-hour out of the city, where young, horny couples went to fuck each other senseless. Typhoon had brought a few girls there himself when he was younger. These days, once the weather grew cold, it was more or less empty. The site was close to the no-man's land between shifter and vampire territory, which made it the perfect place to meet his father.

Typhoon came to a stop and glared at him. He was tall, thin, and gave off the heavy scent of rotten fruit, the smell indicative of a vampire.

"What do you want?" Typhoon snapped as he leaped from his bike. "I told you never to call me."

"Robby, I wouldn't have called if I had any other choice."

The sound of the name his mother had given him sent a growl through his chest. This vampire didn't have the right to talk to him like that, not after everything he'd done.

Typhoon's hands clenched as he glared at the vampire. "I told you never to call me."

His father gazed at him for a long moment and nodded. "I know. And I'm sorry for putting you in this difficult position, but I...I don't have anybody else to call. I've been ousted from Cromwell's kingdom. He caught a family camping in his territory and I—"

"I don't want to hear it." Typhoon bit back the desire to snarl again. He might not want to hear of his father's "heroics," but that didn't mean he could ignore it. If there was someone out with knowledge of vampires, then he had to find them and bring them into the fold, one way or another.

"Fine. What did you do?"

"Got them out." His father scowled and kicked the ground. "The parents and three kids under twelve."

"Human or shifter?"

"Human."

Typhoon shook his head, his grimace deepening. It was always more difficult to deal with humans than shifters when it came to newbies who learned about vampires. A whole family like that would make it even more difficult. The parents were going to be completely freaked out.

"Cromwell found out what I did," his father said, his voice soft and hesitant, “and he exiled me. Once the other kingdoms find out what I did, I’ll have a death warrant on my head.”

“You’re already dead—what difference does it make?”

His father’s shoulders slumped.

Typhoon viewed him for a moment. He looked thinner than normal for a vampire. His skin was even more sunken and pale, with a papery texture. If he didn’t know better, he’d have said it had been several weeks since the vampire had last fed. The sickly scent of rotten fruit seemed stronger on him.

He glanced at his father’s leg. There was a slightly darker area on his pants, making them cling to the leg.

“How long ago was this?”

His father stared at him for a moment before shaking his head. “Three weeks.”

“And you’ve been injured all this time?”

“Yes.”

So it really was desperation that had driven him to call his son. Typhoon snarled under his breath and rolled up his sleeve. His mother’s final words kept playing around in his brain. She had been far more forgiving than his father deserved, but he'd made a promise to her. Now, he'd do whatever it took to keep that promise—to a point.

His father looked exhausted as Typhoon stalked over toward him before shoving his wrist into his father’s face. “Drink.”

"You don't have to—"

"Right. So you'll just end up going into town and killing someone because you've starved yourself? Drink before I change my mind and take you in."

His father took hold of the wrist with a sigh. Typhoon turned his face away, trying to ignore the stab of pain when the fangs punctured his wrist. He could spare a little blood if it meant that innocents in the city—and his father—survived, even if his father's survival wasn't high on his list of priorities.

He waited fifteen minutes while his father drank. When he finally pulled away, Typhoon's legs felt crampy. The rotten-fruit scent had lessened, and his father's face looked a little pinker and much fuller.

“Thanks,” his father said, wiping his mouth.

“Yeah, well, I don’t want some innocent kid in the city ending up dead.”

“You know I don’t—”

Typhoon snorted. All vampires killed. It was a part of who they were. It didn’t matter if they didn’t want to or if it was their policy not to kill. Situations always arose. Starving himself for three weeks? That was one heck of a situation.

Typhoon wrapped his hand around his wrist, stemming the residual blood flow. “We’re done here. Get yourself to another kingdom. Guinevere has been working with us. I doubt she’ll have you killed for intervening on the behalf of children.”

“Robby—”

“If you called thinking that I was going to take you in, you’re crazy. I don’t have room in my life for a vampire, especially not the bastard that killed my mother.”

His father inhaled sharply. A look of pain flashed over his face. Robby was happy to see it. If his father had lived with any of the pain Robby felt every day, knowing his mother was gone and never coming back, then maybe it was a better punishment to leave him alive.

It couldn’t be that much of a punishment if his father were so desperate to live.

“Robby, I never intended—”

Typhoon ripped his arm away from his father’s grasp. His wolf pounded against his chest, and a growl rippled through him. Typhoon's teeth bared. His fangs started to grow. His eyes narrowed.

His father released him at once and backed away, dropping his gaze. It was a reaction with which Typhoon was familiar. He expected it from virtually everyone with whom he interacted. Well, most everyone.

"My name," he said in an even, measured tone, "is Typhoon. Robby was Mom's boy, and he died when she did. I don't care what you intended or what you wanted. You killed her. And it's only because she made me promise not to let you die that I didn't kill you."

His father lifted a tortured gaze, but Typhoon didn't care about his pain. He was the one who had taken his mother away from him. He was the reason she had lain, body broken and bleeding in her son's arms, gasping out her final words, begging him to forgive his father, making him promise not to let his father die while her life slipped away because of him.

"You were never there," Typhoon continued, his voice low. "It was always her and me. You didn't want anything to do with us until she was gone."

"I couldn't stick around, and you know it. It was for your protection. If the Brotherhood knew your mother was involved with a vampire, they'd have turned on her. If they knew you were half-vampire—"

"They'd have killed me. I know. I *know*," Typhoon snarled, "but the Brotherhood was so much smaller back then. There were so many—" He cut himself off. He didn't need to rehash ancient history. Typhoon had gone over it in his mind a million times. He'd screamed and shouted and rained his fists on his father's chest. He'd torn into limbs and broken down, sobbing; there was nothing more to say. "Don't ever call me again. If you do..."

He let the threat hang.

His father didn't reply. Rather, he stood there looking old and tired. Typhoon turned on his heels and marched away before anything else could come of it. Since his father had drunk shifter blood, it would mean he'd be more human for a certain amount of time. He might even be able to pass as human if he made it to the city where he could cling to his humanity by eating a strict vegan diet for a while. He'd eventually revert back to being a vampire, though. He always did, and he always would.

Typhoon had no place for vampires in his life, other than between his jaws. It was his job to protect civilians from vampires, not protect vampires from other vampires. His father had taken care of himself for hundreds of years—he'd be able to take care of himself for a few more hundred years. Typhoon's father wasn't his responsibility.

Don't let him die.

The plea came back to him as Typhoon swung onto his bike and drove away.

The taste of blood welled in his mouth, the remnants of the memories from that day. When he'd come home after running in the woods to find blood scattered throughout his home. When he'd found his mother lying on the floor, her body broken and blood welling from the holes in her neck, the crust of vampire venom building on her pale skin. And his father, lying there next to her.

Up until then, his father had been the guy who'd shown up every few months, stayed overnight only to disappear in the morning. Typhoon had always enjoyed those visits. It was something new, and he liked the way his mother’s eyes lit up whenever his dad was there. He usually brought small gifts with him and plenty of stories.

Then it all changed.

Typhoon had just begun to integrate himself with the Brotherhood. He'd thought if he were part of it, his parents would one day be able to live together without fear. Then he'd come home to find his mother dying, and his father near death. Having been attacked by another vampire and on death’s door, he'd returned to the one person who would always let him in.

And she had.

And he'd lost control.

After his mother had died, Typhoon wanted to kill him. He wanted to tear that vampire apart and leave his body in the street to burn in the sunlight, but his mother’s last words rang in his ears over and over again. Instead, he’d cut his own wrist open and dribbled blood into his father’s mouth until he was strong enough to open his eyes to see what he'd done.

Typhoon's father wept.

He continued to weep until Typhoon kicked him out of the house. Later, he'd returned, trying to get him to go back to wherever he was to live with him, and Typhoon had attacked him. Three years passed before they had any further contact. They'd met in the woods like they had earlier that night.

“Was it you?” he'd asked, staring his father in the eye. “Did you kill her, or was it someone else? Did another vampire do it?”

He wouldn’t have believed his father if he'd said yes, though he would have pretended to. Typhoon had been so young, so alone. He'd wanted anything to give him some semblance of peace again.

But his father hadn’t said yes; he also hadn’t lied.

“No," he'd said. "There was nobody else. It was me, but you have to believe—”

“I don’t have to believe anything,” Typhoon mumbled, just as he had back then.

He'd attacked again. Had nearly killed him. Typhoon had stopped himself just in time. Had spent a week bringing his father back from the brink of death. After that, he told him to leave and never contact him again. His father had broken that rule a handful of times, and each time he did, Typhoon felt that much closer to breaking the promise he'd made to his mother.

Still, if the Brotherhood ever found out he was half-vampire, it’d all be over. There was no way any of them, even the most loyal, would ever accept a half-vampire shifter as their alpha.

His mind flashed to Mia and the look of heady lust in her eyes as he'd pressed her to the wall. It was the least of his concerns, but if she knew his heritage, she'd never want him to touch her again. It was simply a matter of fact. Shifters and vampires were sworn enemies. He'd never be tolerated if the truth of his birth ever got out. Rather, he'd be dead by the end of the week.

Would his father rat him out? Typhoon didn't know. He doubted it, but there was no telling. It wasn't as though he knew the vampire at all.

Typhoon reached the city quickly. He let out a deep breath, and his body relaxed. It was over. His father had been strengthened, and he'd go back on his merry way. In the meantime, Typhoon had to find the family of campers his father had rescued and take care of them. They were his highest priority at the moment.

Mia crossed his mind once more. He couldn't tell her everything that had happened that night, of course, but some information might be necessary. An explanation as to why he had to leave so abruptly, for example.

His phone rang, and Typhoon cursed. If that was him again...

When he pulled to the side of the road to answer, it wasn't his father. It was Twister. "We've had an attack," he yelled over the shouting and pained screams. "We got two vampire bites. Headed for Mia's clinic right now."

Typhoon cursed again. "I'll meet you there."

He hung up and dialed Mia, drumming his fingers against the handles of his bike as he waited, ring by ring. Finally, she answered. "There was an attack," he snapped at her, noting her disgruntled tone but not caring. "Get to the clinic, ASAP."

"I'll be there," Mia promised and hung up.

Typhoon wheeled his bike around, the whole business with his father forgotten—for the time being. There were more important things to do. He revved the engine as he headed for the clinic.

Chapter Five

Mia

Having sent Gracie home earlier, it was impossible to get another sitter on such short notice. Mia hated bringing Jasper to the clinic after a biting attack, but what other choice did she have? She couldn't just leave him at home. No, the best thing to do was to bring him along and get one of the less-wounded men to sit in the car with him while she looked over the injured.

She arrived at the clinic to find a jumble of motorcycles already on the lawn. Her eyes were drawn to the fire-engine red one parked next to the curb. Typhoon was already there. She pulled her car onto the side of the street opposite the clinic and got out. There was a tall, thin shifter waiting outside for her. He loped over as soon as she jumped from the vehicle. It was Harry, one of the shifters she'd trained for on-site first aid. He was a good, trustworthy shifter.

"We have two bites and several chest and abdominal gashes."

Mia nodded as she glanced at him. There wasn't a speck of blood on him. "Were you injured?" she asked, just to make sure.

He shook his head.

"Good." She tossed him her keys. "My son is sleeping in the back. There's a bottle ready for him in the diaper bag if he wakes up. Do *not* bring him into the clinic, understood?"

Harry's eyes widened. "What?"

“If it looks like someone has gone rabid out here, get away. Just drive and leave, understood?” Mia narrowed her eyes at him and put her hands on her hips. “I'm trusting you with my baby's safety. Don't let me down.”

Harry looked at the car nervously, but he swallowed down whatever other protests he might have and nodded bravely. He slid into the car, and Mia took a single moment to doubt herself before turning on her heel. There wasn’t a place for self-doubt. She knew Harry well enough, and it wasn’t like she could bring Jasper into the clinic with her to face whatever violence might be inside.

She raced for the clinic, bursting in to the smell of blood and sweat. It was an even bloodier mess than it had been the night before. Various members moved around, patching up each other’s small wounds. Mia’s gaze swept over them before Typhoon barreled through the doors leading to the examination rooms.

“Hurry,” he snapped at her. “Where do you keep your vamp blood?”

Ingesting vampire blood was the only sure-fire way to neutralize the venom from a vampire bite. It was stomach-churning but better than the alternatives. Mia raced into the back. Even injuries bleeding heavily weren’t as important as vampire bites. If it went untreated for too long, the bitten shifter would turn rabid and kill others. Then it wouldn’t matter who'd been patched-up—everybody was a target.

Typhoon kept on her heels as she unlocked her office and moved to the fridge where the vampire blood was kept. She pulled out a couple of pints and passed them to the alpha, who nodded brusquely and rushed off, and she locked the room again to ensure the others didn't get into the store of drugs she kept onsite. When she was done, Mia raced to help him.

Typhoon was already in the rabid room, where two young-looking shifters were strapped to metal tables that were bolted to the floor. They thrashed as blood foamed at their lips. Mia's gaze slid over their faces. If she knew who they were, she might risk an emotional reaction, and there was no place for emotion right now. She needed to get them taken care of.

"Get away," one of them snarled at Mia as she approached with a nasal tube.

Typhoon had already ripped one of the bags open and was forcing the contents down the shifter's throat, holding his long muzzle open with two fingers inserted between sharp teeth. Mia took a slightly different approach, injecting the second one with drugs to put him out and feeding a tube through his nose and into his stomach before administering the blood. Slowly, the shifters' thrashing ceased.

"Take this," Mia ordered Typhoon, thrusting the bag she'd been holding into his hands. "Since you wasted ninety-percent of that one, I'll have to get more."

He sent her a half-glare but didn't argue. The blood coating the other shifter's face and Typhoon's arms was testament enough to the wastage. Mia ran back to get more bagged blood. She returned to put a nasal tube into the other shifter before pumping the blood directly into his stomach. Both boys soon looked much better.

Mia wiped her hands and turned to the door while Typhoon held both bags up to keep the blood flowing. "I'm going to check on everybody else," she called over her shoulder. "I'll send someone to help."

She rushed back to the main room where pandemonium reigned. Mia leaped onto the front desk, wincing as her braless breasts yanked on her chest and back. She cupped her hands around her mouth and let out a wordless shout to quiet them.

"You." She pointed at Brandon, an eagle shifter she knew relatively well. "Is this everybody?"

"No. We had two men get gut wounds, and I had them taken into rooms one and two already. We're trying to figure out who is worst wounded."

Yet another time when her nurse would have been helpful!

She pointed to an electrocardiographic heart monitor. "Do you know how to use that machine?"

Brandon shook his head.

"Okay. Old school way: check people's pulses. Below sixty beats, they get top priority. If they're spurting blood, tie off the limb as best you can and move them to a room. Anybody who can't answer their names, the date, or their mother's name, come get me. Anybody passes out, come get me. And call 9-11. This is too many people for me to patch up on my own."

There were a few shocked looks from around the room, but Mia didn't waste time on that. Instead, she jumped down and raced to the two rooms where the gut wounds were. The first one wasn't too bad. A lot of blood had drained from of his body, but there were no injuries in the gut itself.

The second one, though...It looked like a vampire had gone to town in his gut with a meat grinder.

Mia grabbed the operating utensils, hooked him up to drugs to put him out and began working to stabilize him. It felt it took hours to clean, stitch, and put things back where they belonged. Her tiger paced, tasting the blood on her tongue. Her patient wasn't going to make it—she sensed it somewhere in the back of her mind. He was bleeding out, and she didn't have the O negative blood for which he'd tested.

The thrill of fear wrapped up her spine as she looked at the pale face. It was Andy. Her hands faltered for the barest moment before the door to the room burst open. Mia jumped, whirling on her heel. A woman in a skin-tight dress and perfect makeup was standing in the doorway, eyes wide and terrified.

Roxy. Andy's sister...and his blood type. She'd donated before.

Mia didn't waste any time explaining. There was no way she'd be able to roll up those sleeves. "Get out of that dress, and sit in the chair next to him."

Thankfully, Roxy didn't argue. She ripped her dress off, even as her mate, Josef, appeared in the doorway behind her. Mia told him what to get from the stores behind her and had him prepare Roxy for giving blood before rounding the table and starting the transfusion.

“As soon as she starts getting pale, close it like this.” She demonstrated by flicking a valve on the transfusion tube. “Understood?”

Josef nodded and crouched down, hands at the ready, while Roxy closed her eyes. The blood pumped from her body into her brother’s, and Mia returned to her work. More blood gushed into her patient's wounds, and she struggled to close it all. At one point, there was the noise of paramedics in the hallway, but Typhoon’s deep, rumbling voice prevented them from interrupting her.

By the time Mia had finished and let herself glance at the clock again, it was nearly five in the morning. She swayed on her feet as she went out to speak with Roxy and Josef, both of whom she had sent away as soon as Roxy could give no more. They stood glaring at Typhoon. Tears coursed down Roxy's face.

Mia marched between them, ignoring the tension in the air. "Josef, take Roxy home to your baby. Andy won't benefit by having her fall down."

"I'm not going anywhere," Roxy snapped.

There was no point in arguing that. "Fine. Take a room, get some sleep. Everybody else was moved to the hospital?"

Typhoon frowned at her. “Yes. I’m going to have one hell of a time explaining this one, though.”

“Explain away, I don’t give a damn.” Mia glared at him. “If I hadn’t had the humans called in, we’d have had deaths. Hell, Andy still isn’t out of the woods. One person isn’t enough to deal with all this. Now, I have to go check on my son.”

She stormed out of the clinic, exhaustion breaking through her body.

Harry was sitting in the back seat, holding an empty bottle and looking utterly exhausted. Relief broke over his face when he saw her. Mia thanked him and brought Jasper into the clinic. When she started to yawn, Roxy silently took the car seat and grasped Mia’s arm.

“Go get showered and get some rest yourself. Josef and I will look after the baby.”

Mia was too tired to argue. She nodded. Mia checked on the two bite victims, to find them resting peacefully, and she made her way to the shower. After she'd stripped down and stepped into the warm water, she thought about curling up in the small space at the bottom of the shower and taking a soggy nap. Just as she'd decided to do it, there was the noise of the door opening.

Through the filmy curtain around the shower she saw a hulking form that could only belong to Typhoon. “I’m joining you,” he rumbled.

Mia thought about sending him away on principle alone. He didn’t get to just decide these things on his own!

However, left on her own, she was afraid she might fall over, so she scooted over a little and opened the curtain invitingly.

Typhoon undressed. Dark bruises circled his eyes. Mia admired his body, feeling distant and unattached to her own.

When he stepped in, and his body brushed against hers, she was well aware of the feel of his skin on hers.

Typhoon pressed her against the wall, his gaze deep, dark, and demanding. His hands clasped her hips and pulled her forward, telling her—without words—exactly what he was about to do with her body.

Heat coiled in her core. Tingles brushed over her skin. Her lips parted slightly.

Typhoon leaned forward, lingering inches from her lips. "He fucked up."

"What?" It was the last thing Mia expected to hear. Her hands curled around Typhoon's thick biceps, only half-hearing what he was saying.

"Twister. He fucked up. Big time. I tell him he doesn't have the necessities to be an alpha, and he immediately rounds up his gang and goes after a coven hidden in the city. Of course, his sister and Hurricane blame me for it. He wasn't supposed to do that." Typhoon pressed his forehead to hers and closed his eyes. The shower ran over his head, plastering his dark hair to his skull and dripping over his face and onto hers. "And what's even worse: I'm going to have to oust him."

Mia gasped. "You can't be serious."

Typhoon's hands gripped her hips more tightly. "Being alpha means I have to make the hard decisions. This was *his* fault. *His* stupidity. Please." The word sounded so alien on his lips, it silenced Mia's protests. "You're not my mate. I don't want a mate. But right now, I want to be inside you. I want to fuck you until I can't tell where you start and I end."

He opened his mouth again, desire and a rare vulnerability raging in his eyes. Mia's hands tightened around his neck. Her gaze pierced into his. She nodded, without saying a word. The lengthy operation, the fear of losing a patient and a friend, and so much more had built up in her, and she wanted that peace of mind, too. She'd never seen Typhoon like this before, and she had the feeling she never would again.

A soft, shuddering sigh escaped Typhoon's lips. His tight grip on her hips loosened, and he started to move his hands up and down her body, tracing over her wet skin. His fingers played over her soft stomach, hid beneath her heavy breasts, tested the strength of her ass. Mia kept her hands on his biceps, thinking that if she moved too quickly, he'd fly away like a bird, and she'd never touch him again.

His lips were hesitant against hers, even as the heat swirled hotter in her core. Mia slowly brought her arms up to wrap them around his neck, then dug her fingers into his hair and pulled him down closer. His tongue breached her mouth, and it was like a whole different person took over.

Mia gasped as Typhoon pushed her against the back wall of the shower.

One of his hands moved to her thigh, lifting it over his hip as his lips curled back into a snarl. His huge body pressed against hers. His length rubbed against her clit as he ground into her. She felt him getting bigger and harder, and she stifled her gasp with another kiss.

He reached beside them and turned the water to a cooler temperature. Mia shivered at first, but as he lifted her, continuing to grind against her clit, she understood why. Heat flashed over her skin. It sizzled at the edges and sunk deep into her flesh. She cried out, then immediately slapped a hand over her mouth as her cheeks turned bright red.

Typhoon grinned at her, adjusting her so he could slide a finger into her. A shudder racked down her spine. She clung tighter to him and let out another strangled cry.

"Let yourself go. Make a little noise," he told her.

Mia shook her head and glared at him, which was hard to do with his large finger sliding in and out of her and his thumb lazily circling her clit. "They'll hear," she hissed

"Roxy and Hurricane are passed out," Typhoon replied, raising a brow. "And so is everybody else in this clinic. I locked the front door. If the baby wakes up, he's got people to take care of him. You don't have to worry about making a little noise."

Well, since he'd said it in that tone, she wasn't about to make a single noise. Served him right, too! She pressed her lips together resolutely and shook her head.

Typhoon paused, making her tense, and then he pulled away from her.

"What are you doing?" she cried out.

Typhoon jumped, startled, then chuckled. "I thought you wanted me to stop."

"When did I say that?"

He shrugged. "Guess when you shook your head, I took it as a no."

Mia harrumphed. Since he wasn't touching her anymore, she started to rub her body against his, sighing in delight when his hardness connected with her clit at just the right angle. "I was saying no to making a lot of noise."

Typhoon groaned. His eyes pinched shut for a moment, then he pushed her against the wall again. His mouth came to hers, crashing together in a series of snarls and groans as he thrust madly against her, as though he were already inside. The friction sent bolts of pleasure shooting through her body so strongly, she couldn't help but cry out again while clinging to him for support.

"If you won't make noise," he growled, "then I will!"

He was true to his word. Mia clawed at his back as he took a step back and entered in one swift thrust, sending bursts of pleasure tinged with the slightest bit of pain. Somehow, the stitch of pain made the whole thing that much more pleasurable. He continued to thrust, lips curled back from his teeth, his growls growing louder and louder.

Mia stared into his glittering eyes as he battered her body, the cold water spraying between them. Her core tightened and throbbed. Her cries came almost as swiftly as his.

Typhoon dropped his forehead to hers, pressed a long kiss to her lips, and drew forward a howl.

Mia's back arched. Her head slammed against the shower, only to come forward and slam back. This time, Typhoon caught it in one hand and pulled her closer to him. Her whole body writhed, and yet somehow, he continued to hold her up as though she weighed nothing.

He thrust harder, his teeth nipping at her shoulder. “Scream for me, darling. Scream my name.”

Mia was only too happy to obey. All the muscles inside of her clamped down and what small hold she had on reality fleeted away. She screamed his name, again and again as first one wave poured over her and then another and another. Her arms went limp, her spine sagged, and Typhoon grunted. He pressed her against the wall again, his thrusts becoming gentler and gentler until he slowly lowered her back down. She could hardly support herself as she panted and shoved her sopping hair away from her eyes.

He withdrew, and she whimpered from loss. Her widened when she saw that he was still hard. “You didn’t finish.”

"We don't have a condom." He grunted as he took himself in one hand. "Don't want to get you pregnant."

"But—" You already have once, she thought.

Mia swallowed her protest as Typhoon grunted and pumped himself with one hand. Her mind whirled, so high on her pleasure and the shock from the memory that she didn't mind his making her do little more than stand and watch while he finished himself off, grunting and tensing as spurts came from him and disappeared down the drain.

When he was done, Typhoon kissed her gently once more. He picked up a bar of soap from where it sat in a rack. "Thank you," he whispered, "for taking care of my men and me. Let me take care of you, now." He winked as he turned her around and washed her back. "Like a true sugar daddy does."

Mia opened her mouth, then closed it again. She was silent as he cleaned her, unable to make her brain settle on anything. She had to tell him, right? But he didn't want to have a child, that much was clear. Mia throbbed between her legs still, but she closed her eyes and tried not to feel his hand on her body as he cleaned her.

She had three shifters almost dead out there. She had to get out before it was her lying on the table. Or worse, it might be Jasper one day.

Chapter Six

Typhoon

Mia fell asleep shortly after he'd carried her, freshly cleaned, dried, and wearing an extra set of scrubs, to one of the unoccupied rooms and put her to bed. Just before she'd drifted off, she asked sleepily for Jasper, but Typhoon was content to let Roxy and Hurricane take care of the baby. They had experience, having a young one themselves, and Mia needed her sleep after being up all hours of the night.

The clinic bed was a little larger than standard hospital beds, as shifters were naturally a little larger than humans. There wasn't that much extra room, but Typhoon managed to squeeze in next to her as she slept. He had to admit, there was something nice about holding her in his arms, inhaling her scent, and seeing the way her whole body relaxed in sleep.

He buried his face in her hair and inhaled. The scent of shampoo and soap wasn't quite enough to overpower her natural scents; she smelled wild and untamed, full of power and vitality. It was her scent that had drawn him to her in the first place. A slight chill ran down his spine, a recognition that he shouldn't have gone to get her the night before, the way he had.

Typhoon had a system. He could smell when a woman was on birth control, and he never slept with one who wasn't. He always used a condom, too. Accidental pregnancy was something he couldn't risk, not with his heritage. As a half-vampire, he knew his own past, and that was that. He'd grown from infancy to full-aged in a year, and he hadn't had the luxury of keeping a child's mind, either. Sure, there were some things he could only have learned by experience but looking back on his life, he wasn't immature mentally, even when he had been physically. In fact, in many ways, it felt like he never was a child.

How would it affect a baby to have a half-shifter, half-vampire child?

And yet, he'd gone to Mia, even though he could smell she wasn't on birth control, and he didn't have a condom. He'd just craved the forgetfulness that sex would bring, even more than he had earlier in the day, after the phone call with his father. He breathed deeply of her scent, which overpowered the other scents in the clinic, the blood, the antiseptics, and everything else.

He knew that he wouldn't be able to put it off indefinitely. He didn't sleep as he held her—rather, he merely used her to ground himself. Why her? He wasn't certain. There was just something calming about being with Mia. Maybe it was due to the fact she refused to put up with his bullshit, and she wasn't afraid of ordering him around when necessary.

When he heard stirring in the other rooms, Typhoon knew he could put it off no longer. His stomach cramped. Twister was a good member of the Brotherhood. He was in it for the right reasons. But last night? That could not be ignored. And if Typhoon ever forgave such a serious transgression...?

He slipped away from Mia, pausing when she stirred. Fortunately, she settled back down quickly. He didn't want to involve her in this, not after all the work she'd put into keeping Twister alive.

Typhoon pulled on his shirt—which he hadn’t bothered to put on after the shower he'd shared with Mia—and left the room. He thought about checking on the others, but that would give him one more excuse to delay the inevitable, so he headed straight to the room where Twister had been left to recover. The sound of a heart monitor greeted him when he stepped in, as did Twister's wary, exhausted eyes.

Twister lay awake in the bed, looking as though he had just woken. His expression was especially grim, a haunted look mingled with regret. When his gaze shifted to Typhoon, he flinched. “Did anybody die?” Twister asked. His breath was short, and it was clear he was in a lot of pain.

Typhoon shook his head. “Not this time. We had to call in the human doctors, though. There was too much for Mia to handle. She spent a good five hours on you, alone.”

Twister nodded slightly, looking relieved for a moment before his face darkened. “Are you going to kill me?”

That was the question, wasn’t it? Typhoon had gotten a report from the others in Twister’s gang about the events from the previous night. They had been furious—furious, worried, and uncertain. Twister had messed up, big time. Going after a vampire coven in the city without prior permission wasn’t too large a transgression. Getting his men hurt made it worse, but it was their job to root out vampires.

No, it was the events taking place at the coven that made this so bad.

"I haven't decided yet." Typhoon shook his head as he brought a chair to sit beside Twister; it was what he hated most about being alpha. "I told you that when you're alpha, you have to make hard choices, but I'll give you a chance to tell your side of what happened."

Twister nodded slowly. He turned his gaze to the ceiling and stared at it for a long time. Eventually, he swallowed. "There were children."

"And?"

"I thought that if I were able to take out the vampires, you'd have no choice but to admit I have more potential than you've realized. I gathered my men, and we set out, but when we got there...there were children, and a vampire threw himself onto his knees and begged us not to hurt them." Twister's expression darkened. "Like an idiot, I called for my men to stand down and tried to negotiate, but it was a trap. The vampires came out of nowhere, and we were surrounded. I don't even know what happened to the kids."

Typhoon put a hand on his shoulder, awkwardly trying to comfort him. "They got out. They were being held as prisoners."

Twister shook his head, self-disgust masking his features. "I was an idiot, and I nearly got my people killed over...I just thought that maybe these vampires weren't so bad. Maybe they were more like Queen Guinevere, but I was wrong."

"Luckily for you, you were the one who was closest to being killed."

Twister turned to face him again, frowning. "I know Luke and Hans were both bitten."

"We got vamp blood into them in time. They ought to be waking up soon." Typhoon cocked his head as he studied the other shifter. He saw regret in Twister's face, but also, bravery—he wasn't about to flinch, whatever Typhoon proclaimed his punishment to be.

"You broke trust, Twister. You put your men's lives in danger for the sake of a vampire. Regardless of what I decide, do you really think they'll continue to follow you after this?"

A flash of anger broke on Twister's face. He made to sit, but his injuries hadn't healed enough for him to do much more than whimper and fall back against the pillows. His face turned a sickly shade of green, and he screwed his eyes tightly shut.

“I didn’t do anything for the sake of a vampire,” he spat. “I was thinking of the children. I thought they might have been the vampire’s kids; they didn’t deserve to see their father die if that were the case! And the vampire...I didn’t *know* he was holding them prisoner. If he'd genuinely been taking care of them, protecting them—”

“It’s not your call to make when it comes to vampires.”

Twister opened his eyes again, still looking furious. What, exactly, he was furious about, Typhoon wasn’t sure. “But it’s our call to be executioners, to decide they don’t deserve mercy, no matter who we face.”

“You’re having a crisis.”

“Are you saying I shouldn’t? That I shouldn’t wonder if all this killing is really necessary every single damn time? Are you telling me you've never once, in your long years as Alpha of the Brotherhood, looked into the eyes of a vampire and wondered if they were actually evil?”

Typhoon’s mind flashed to his father. His sad, dark eyes, so much like Typhoon’s own. They looked like each other, that much was clear. His father’s features seemed hardened on Typhoon. His father's stature was slimmer and shorter than his son’s, but that didn’t change the fact that it wouldn’t take much for people to realize they were related.

“Of course, I have,” Typhoon replied softly, a flash of regret passing through him. “And I had to learn a painful lesson about vampires, too. They aren’t evil. No more than humans or shifters are evil.”

Twister’s eyes widened.

“But that doesn’t matter.”

“How can it not—”

“They're too dangerous. They can’t be trusted. Even those who want to do good, like Guinevere. We can’t know for certain what they really want, and even if we did, how well can they control themselves? Do you think every vampire-caused death was on purpose?”

Twister sank back into his bed, looking exhausted. “There has to be another way, something that doesn’t keep killing people, something that doesn’t put our own people in danger.”

It was comments like that that helped Typhoon decide Twister wasn't suited to be an alpha, though he never thought he'd go out and nearly get himself killed, proving him right.

“I didn’t expect you to be soft on the vampires. Especially not with what happened to your parents.”

Twister flinched. “My parents wouldn’t want their deaths to be used as the basis of reckless hate. And it’s not like I'm giving out love balloons to vampires, besides. In this particular case, I just thought I saw a different way, and I don’t want to see any more good men die when there might be another way! What's so wrong with that?”

“Nothing, unless you're putting more good men in danger of dying because of it; which you did.”

Typhoon viewed him for a long time. It was true that in the last few years he’d been a little softer on certain actions than he should've been. That whole mess with Thunder and his little kitty-mate had started it. But she’d been pregnant *and* his mate. It was something that was understandable to the majority of the Brotherhood.

This, though? This wasn’t something anybody could understand. There was the chance the members of the Brotherhood would go after Twister for what he did. His men had been confused and betrayed by his actions, and they hovered between throwing him under the bus and sticking up for him. It wasn't a position they—or the rest of the gang, for that matter—should be caught up in.

"It's too bad that you were such an idiot. The Brotherhood could use more people in it that joined for the reasons you did." Typhoon shook his head as he stood. "It'd be a shame to waste so much of Mia's work by killing you, so, no, I won't be killing you. Not today, at least. But you're too soft for this."

Twister stared at him, alarm seeping into his eyes.

"I can't have a leader out there that I can't trust. Not to mention that your men can't trust you anymore. So you'll be stripped of your position."

"I can prove myself again."

Typhoon viewed him with pity. He knew what was coming; it shone clearly from his eyes. The pleading in his gaze was more than enough to prove Twister knew that losing his position was the least of his punishment.

"You will also be ousted from the Brotherhood. We don't have a place for someone who puts his brothers at risk, not on any level. I will put out the word that you are off limits, so you don't have to worry about anybody coming after you, but you are no longer welcome in any safe house, at meetings, or anyplace the Brotherhood gathers. If you breach these rules, only you can be held responsible for what happens to you afterward."

Twister gasped. "You can't." He struggled with the wires stuck to his body and his own weakness. "You can't throw me out. I can prove myself again. I learned my lesson. I—"

"No, you didn't." Typhoon shook his head. Even though he wished that there was another way, it was the best thing for the Brotherhood, which was his main concern. He liked Twister and was sad to see him go, but in the end, he'd brought it on himself. "If you'd learned your lesson, you wouldn't be arguing about there being other ways. You'd understand this is it."

Twister shook his head. "Please. Without the Brotherhood, I don't have anything. I've given my whole life to—"

"You should have thought about that before you betrayed us."

Twister froze, then crumpled. He turned his face away and closed his eyes. He sucked in a deep breath, and his muscles slowly relaxed. Twister didn't speak again. He didn't look at Typhoon, but he nodded tersely.

Typhoon opened his mouth, wanting to tell him that if he worked hard enough, he might one day prove himself worthy to return to the Brotherhood, but that would be a lot of hard work, and it would, more than likely, end up with him dead.

There weren't many people who, once ousted from the Brotherhood, ever found a way back in. There were a few, like Hurricane and Blizzard, who managed to stay at the fringes, helping out from time to time. They were almost a part of it, but they could never be true members again. Best not put ideas in Twister's head that might end up with him being killed.

"I'll go wake your sister so she can take you home."

Twister's eyes widened. "Roxy's here?"

"She gave you blood." Typhoon paused a moment, then shook his head. "You were an idiot, Twister, a real idiot."

He stalked from the room and went to wake Roxy and Hurricane. The baby was sound asleep in his car seat, and there was the faint odor of a dirty diaper. At first, Typhoon was afraid it was still attached to the baby, but then he spied the diaper in the trash. As Roxy and Hurricane collected Twister—promising to get him his own personal nurse for him while recovering—Typhoon carried the car seat to Mia's room.

The baby squirmed a little before settling down again. Mia breathed peacefully, a small smiled on her face. Whatever she must be dreaming was better than the reality that would face her when she woke.

Typhoon looked between them for a long moment, but as Jasper's eyes began to flutter, he quickly made his exit. The desire to talk to his own father had hit him hard and unexpectedly. Their brief talk the previous night played over in his head.

Vampires were evil; not the person, perhaps, but the being. They couldn't control their bloodlust.

Twister's words kept ringing through his mind, and Typhoon couldn't help but wonder as he pulled out his phone...

Was there another way?

Chapter Seven

Mia

Roxy stopped into the room to tell her they were leaving. Mia protested because Andy shouldn't be traveling yet, but Roxy told her Typhoon had told them to leave, and they would leave before he did anything that made her honor-bound to kill him. After checking him over one last time, Mia reluctantly agreed that Andy was stable enough to travel so long as they used an ambulance. She checked in on the two who had been bitten and found them awake. By then, Jasper had let her know that he was awake and ready to start the day.

Mia carried Jasper in one arm, letting him nurse while she did a quick examination of the two shifters who had been bitten.

“How are you feeling?” she asked. She checked each of their heart rates.

The one on the left, Stephen, grunted. “Well enough, considering I got bitten by one of those fucking vampires. What was Twister even thinking?”

Mia shook her head. She didn’t know the details of what had happened, and she didn’t want to know, either. “That isn’t any of my business. My business is to keep you lot alive.”

Stephen grumbled while she finished the examination. As was her experience since Guinevere had revealed the trick to feed bitten shifters vampire blood, they appeared to be in perfect health.

"I think the two of you are free to leave. You're not showing any danger signs. I'll call someone to come pick you up."

Stephen nodded tersely at her. Mia exited the room, plucked Jasper from her breast, and held him to her shoulder. She covered herself and patted his back. He fussed and squirmed until a large burp came out before settling back down. Mia brought him to her other breast, already looking forward to sitting while she made the call.

She reached the waiting room, and the distinctive scent of cigarette smoke wafted in through the window. Mia growled and marched for the door. How many times did she have to tell these idiots that there was no smoking on her premises? She charged outside, ready to start yelling, but was brought up short when a soft voice reached her ears.

“I don’t know if I can.”

The voice turned harsh. “You don’t think I know that? You don’t think I know that you wish things had been different?” She was shocked when she realized the voice belonged to Typhoon. His tone dropped again, going back to that same soft, pleading, vulnerable tone. The same tone he'd used the previous night, she realized. “It’s not that simple. It happened. Regardless of what either of us wants, it happened. I can’t just stop hating you because...because I want to. I don’t want to, anyway. I don’t want to forgive you.”

Who was he talking to that had him sounding so distraught?

Mia inched closer to the corner of the building until she could just see Typhoon's shoes peeking out from around the edge. She cradled Jasper in both arms and held her breath. Typhoon was so involved in his call that he didn't notice. There was another blast of cigarette smoke, and he rose his voice again.

"Because you killed—" He cut off, and Mia saw him stiffen.

Her heart jumped to her throat, certain he'd caught her eavesdropping. Part of her wanted to rush back to the clinic, but her tiger snarled at her weakness. Instead, she took a few great strides and rounded the corner as though she hadn't been stalking up on him at all.

"Put that smelly thing out at once," she ordered, pointing at the cigarette. "People are trying to breathe, here!"

Typhoon growled as he started. He slammed his finger into the cell phone, turning it off at once before stuffing it into his pocket. "I'll do whatever the hell I want!"

His roar almost made Mia flinch. It made Jasper jerk, and he flailed about, exposing her breasts for the world to see as he screamed. Mia hastily buttoned two more buttons to cover herself and held her baby to her shoulder, bouncing him. She glared at Typhoon as he took another drag on the cigarette. He stared her in the eye as he did.

"Put that out," Mia hissed. "Do you want to give yourself cancer?"

“Shifters don’t get cancer.”

“It’s rare, but it does happen.” Mia slapped the cigarette from his hand and stomped on it. “There is no smoking near my clinic. You know the rules. I’ve told them to you often enough. If you’re not going to obey them, then get on that bike of yours and leave.”

Typhoon glowered at her and snorted. “Well, I guess that’s one thing to look forward to after you quit. I won’t have to put up with your goody-two-shoes ways anymore.”

Mia opened her mouth, then closed it again. She was going to quit—hadn't the night before been proof enough that she couldn’t keep doing this? Just bringing Jasper to the clinic was a danger in itself. She had to put him first above anything else.

She wondered if Twister would still be alive if she hadn't been the one at the clinic.

Mia sucked in a breath to calm herself as she continued soothing Jasper. He was calming down quickly enough, twisting his body (flopping around in her arms in the process) to peer intensely at Typhoon. Typhoon peered back at her with the same eyes, and her stomach dropped. Anybody looking at the two of them could plainly see they were father and son. Anybody.

"I'm sending the two who were bitten home," she blurted, shielding Jasper from Typhoon's gaze. "Thought you might want to talk to them first."

"I don't."

"Okay, fine. Just...don't light up another cigarette," she said as the ambulance to take Twister to Hurricane's house pulled into the parking lot. "Otherwise, I'm going to beat your ass."

A faint smile spread over Typhoon's face at that. "Hmm. I might like that."

Whatever anger he had over her having listened to his conversation had gone, or he was simply redirecting her. It worked—the image of her dressed in leathers, holding a whip as she straddled him tied to a bed with a ball in his mouth came to her mind, and heat rushed to her cheeks. She almost told him not to say such things in front of her baby, but she was certain her voice would only come out a squeak.

The paramedics got out of the ambulance. Mia turned on her heel and marched over to them. She directed them inside and oversaw Andy's transfer to the ambulance. Roxy and Josef stuck close by. Mia rubbed her neck and adjusted Jasper who had started to root around for more food.

Just as the ambulance, Roxy, and Josef had left the parking lot, another car came in—a sleek Lexus. Blake stepped out of it. His eyes seemed to burn with anger, and Mia bit back a curse. Stephen must have called them; they were close friends, from what she had seen.

No, there hadn't been time for Stephen to call him. He must have found out some other way.

Blake ignored Mia and the clinic, charging right for Typhoon instead. "Bastard!"

Typhoon shifted his stance stopping Blake in his tracks. “And what am I a bastard for this time, Hailstorm?” he snarled loudly.

Blake’s muscles bunched. His hands clenched into fists, and he bore his teeth with a snarl. “Twister’s hide should be hanging from a wall already, yet you let him drive out of here without any consequences.”

Mia backed toward the clinic. Whatever had happened the night before must have been very terrible for Blake to be so angry and defiant over it. Her heart started to beat a little faster, and she pulled Jasper closer to her chest. The only two left there besides Typhoon were the shifters who’d been bitten. Which side would land on?

"There *are* consequences," Typhoon said, but Mia could see that Blake was beyond words.

She turned on her heel and dashed into the clinic, running straight to her locked storeroom. She unlocked it, placed Jasper on the floor where he wouldn't get into anything, and locked the room again before dashing outside to hear a roar met with a cry of pain. When she raced out the door, she found Blake and Typhoon at each other's throats, fists flying as dark fur spread over their bodies and sharp teeth grew in their mouth.

Stephen and the other one were soon behind her, asking what was going on. Mia wasted no time explaining.

Blake jabbed a fist into Typhoon's kidneys, and Typhoon reached to snap

Blake’s neck. Mia dodged into the thick of it. Both of her fists flew out. One palm slammed into Blake’s nose and the other into Typhoon’s.

Twin cracks rang out through the air. Both men stumbled back. Blood burst from Blake’s nose; it spurted from Typhoon’s. Both stared at her with a mix of rage and shock. Mia snarled, bringing her tiger closer to the surface. They might be big wolves, but she was a big cat. She could easily trounce them both in her tiger form.

Well, maybe not easily, but she could still do it.

“That's enough of you acting like children,” she shouted, making sure to include both of them in her glare. “Nobody's getting killed at my clinic.”

"*Your* clinic," Blake sneered. "Is that why Twister got let off without a hook? Or is it because you sucked off the alpha and got him in a nice, agreeable state to do whatever you wanted? Got him begging you for more?"

Mia rolled her eyes. If he was trying to upset her, accusing her of having sex (especially to someone who was technically her husband) wasn't the way to do it. "If you're here to pick Stephen up, he's free to go. Clean bill of health. I suggest you leave now."

"Hiding behind a woman?" Blake turned his sneer to Typhoon. "Should have known the moment you bought her. You're spineless, and binding yourself to one woman—especially one as old and fat as her—"

"Hey!" Mia started forward, a growl on her lips.

Typhoon caught her by the elbow. "Leave him to me."

She turned to tell him that she could take care of herself, and caught the flash of movement in her eye. Blake lunged forward, claws extending from his nailbeds, and pain blossomed across her shoulders, causing her to fall forward into Typhoon's arms.

Two shouts echoed from behind her. As she clung to Typhoon, white-hot pain throbbing in her shoulders, there was a third shout. More claws dug into her, and Typhoon spun her out of the way.

The claws tore free, causing her to scream, and her tiger raced to the surface, hovering just below her skin.

Typhoon seized Blake by the throat and kicked his feet out from under him. Mia fell to her knees, hot blood scorching a path down her back. Stephen and the other shifter rushed to her. She tried to assure them she was okay, but her eyes were still locked on Typhoon and Blake. Typhoon's hands were locked around Blake's neck, his face rapidly turning red.

"Typhoon," she gasped, "no."

The alpha's eyes blazed. For a dreadful moment, Mia thought he would ignore her and kill Blake anyway. But then, slowly, as if he were fighting himself, Typhoon released his grip on Blake's throat.

The shifter coughed. His face still red, he shoved Typhoon.

The alpha got to his feet and sent a vicious kick into Blake's stomach.

Mia cried out in protest as Blake doubled over double, his red face quickly turning to a sickly shade of green.

"Consider yourself lucky, dog," Typhoon growled at him. "The only reason I will not kill you now is because the doctor doesn't want bloodshed at her clinic. You'd best take the chance to run while you can. The next time we meet, you will not be so fortunate."

He turned on his heel and strode over to Mia. The other two shifters scattered, rushing back to the clinic walls and standing there, looking uncertain and afraid. Typhoon's furious, hard expression melted into concern as he knelt beside Mia and put a hand on her shoulder.

“Are you all right?” he asked, his voice low.

Stephen skirted them and went to Blake’s side.

Mia glared at the wolf that had attacked her while her back had been turned. She would shed no tears for him, but she still felt like it was necessary to fight for him. Blood still trickled down her back as her mind shot to Jasper, alone on the floor in a locked room. Anxiety seized her innards, and she grabbed Typhoon’s arm.

“Take me inside.”

Typhoon picked her up and turned to the clinic. Stephen helped Blake to his feet, while the other shifter nearly tripped over himself to open the door for Typhoon.

Blake laughed a loud, raucous laughter, full of bitterness and hate. “I should've known this would happen. Typhoon, alpha of the Savage Brotherhood, has gone and got himself whipped.”

A growl reverberated in Typhoon’s chest, but he didn’t turn back.

“There was a time when you took care of this gang,” Blake continued shouting.

Mia flinched. If the fighting hadn’t already gotten the attention of the neighbors, his shouting certainly would. The last thing she needed was the cops gumming up the clinic—again. They made it a habit of stopping by regularly, hoping to catch her off-guard so they could have something on her or her patients to arrest them.

“What’s the matter,” Blake shouted again, “cat got your tongue, Typhoon?” The door swung shut, but not before his last words rang through the air. “Has she even told you that brat of hers is yours?”

Typhoon froze. Mia’s breath locked in her chest as her head whipped around to stare into his eyes. His arms tightened as disbelief flickered over his face. He must've seen the truth in her expression because a storm cloud descended over him and he let out a deep, threatening growl.

“What is he talking about?”

Chapter Eight

Typhoon

"I wasn't going to tell you."

Fear shone from Mia's eyes, but she lifted her chin in a defiantly and glared at him. Her arms were around his neck, her weight warm in his arms. Outside, the two shifters were hurrying Hailstorm away, probably hoping he wouldn't shift and turn on them.

Idiots. As if he'd do anything like that in broad daylight when there were witnesses.

Typhoon locked the door with one hand, then carried Mia to one of the examination rooms. He dropped her on the examination table, ignoring her wince, and glared at her.

"What the fuck is this?"

Mia shoved him away and got to her feet shakily. “Jasper needs me.”

He reached for her arm to stop her, but the baby was crying. Typhoon stepped back to let her get up and followed her to the supply room. Her hands shook as she unlocked the door. Blood stained her scrubs, and from her hitched breathing, he knew she was in pain. He couldn’t make himself help her, though, not even when she opened the door to find the baby half-stuck under a shelf.

“Are you okay?” Mia quickly collected her child and pulled him into a protective embrace. “Shh, it’s okay. Mommy’s got you.”

She peeked over her shoulder at him, fear still in her eyes. He wanted to be angry that she was frightened of him, but he couldn't decide his dominant emotion. All he could do was stand there and glower at her.

The scent of blood worked its way into his brain, and Typhoon shook his head. He grasped Mia's elbow, led her back to the examination room, and yanked some cleaners and gauze from a small cabinet.

"Take off your shirt," he grunted at her.

Mia sat on the bed and stared at him. "You're not going to say anything?"

"About what?"

"You really want to play games right now?"

Typhoon dropped the supplies on the bed beside her. "What's there to say?

He's talking out of his ass. You were on birth control, and we used a condom."

Mia's nostrils flared. "Yeah, and I still ended up with a baby. The chances were one in a million. The birth control I used was ninety-nine percent effective, and condoms are ninety-eight percent effective. Together, there should've been no chance, and yet..."

A cold, slimy feeling slithered up his throat. "So you're saying that I could have other children out there?"

"Not likely."

"But it wasn't *likely* for you to get pregnant!" Typhoon snarled. His hands shook, but he refused to look at the baby in her arms. It was impossible. Mia and Blake must have come up with this scheme together for some reason. They were trying to topple him...something! "I don't have any interest in being a father."

"I know," she snapped back, "and that's why I wasn't going to tell you."

Typhoon wheeled for the door. Maybe he should feel bad for leaving her wounded, but she could take care of herself. His lungs seemed no longer able to expand, and he couldn't get his brain to work properly. This whole notion was so ludicrous, he wanted to laugh. Instead, his stomach twisted itself into knots, and he could hardly see what was around him.

Blake and the others were gone when he got outside; good for them. If they'd still been around, he might not have been able to contain his temper, but it also meant that by the end of the day, everybody would know about the possibility that he had a child.

But it wasn't a possibility, was it? He nearly laughed at himself as he raced to where his bike had been parked. If it weren't true, Mia wouldn’t have been so afraid, so it was real because she was afraid of what his reaction would be. And she should be afraid of him! He was a dangerous man. He was half-vampire. There was evil in his blood, and nothing was going to change that.

His stomach wrapped in yet another knot as he thought of the small baby in her arms. How old was Jasper? Four months? Were babies usually that big at four months? Was it normal for a four-month-old to wriggle around on the floor and get stuck beneath shelves? Was it usual to have that intelligent gaze in a baby’s eyes? Did the baby know that

Typhoon was his father just by looking at him?

Typhoon's own memories from when he was that small were hazy, but they were still there. He remembered the discomfort of wet and dirty diapers and the frustration at not being able to tell his mother what was wrong with him. He hadn't experienced things in thoughts as much as pure feeling, but thought had come quickly. He'd also fully grown in a single year; he'd had to eat almost constantly and was always in pain, his body feeling like it was stretching out. There were days when all he could do was lie in bed, watch documentaries, and wish he was going to die.

Was that the future that Jasper faced? Was he already growing faster than he should be? Was Mia terrified about what might happen to her child as she watched him getting bigger every day?

Typhoon wove through traffic, the air currents of the vehicles around him brushing his hair. He became aware that his helmet was still hanging from one side of the handlebars, but he didn’t stop to put it on.

Hadn't he just thought the drama with his father was all he'd have to deal with right then?.

His head brushed against a driver’s side mirror. Horns honked loudly as he pressed between two neck-in-neck cars. Finally, adrenaline kicked in to cut out the thoughts from his head. It was just at the right point; he'd driven until the bike was running on fumes, and he finally stopped to fill it up. As soon as he didn't have the driving to concentrate on, the thought he'd been avoiding flashed into his mind.

He had to tell Mia. She had to know his heritage—her son's heritage. He had to tell her everything. How the hell was he meant to do that?

Typhoon could just imagine how she'd react to it—by putting a scalpel through his throat. That's what he'd do if their places had been reversed.

What he didn't know was what all this meant for Jasper. His throat seized up. If Mia rejected the baby, would he have to take him and run? Would he give up everything in order to care for a child he'd never wanted? Had he once wanted to be a father? Hadn't he given up on that line of thinking when his mom had died? He had to take responsibility for

Jasper, didn't he? It was the only right thing to do.

Having finished filling his tank, Typhoon jumped back on his bike and headed for the woods. He needed to run, to burn off his excess energy and put his thoughts in order, rather than block them from his mind. He wasn't going to figure any of it out if he didn't work it through.

Soon, he was up in the mountain paths, breathing the clean air as he navigated the rocky roads. Being away from the noise of the city helped to settle his racing pulse and clear his head. He didn't have to tell Mia everything right away. All he had to do was find out how quickly Jasper was developing. If he were growing up faster than expected, Mia would have expressed some concerns about that, wouldn't she? So, he must be more or less normal—

Something shot out from the trees. It rammed into the side of the bike, and Typhoon lost control. He was flung from the bike, thrown headfirst at the road. Typhoon managed to shift and twist in the air to hit the ground with a roll and come to a stop on the side of the road.

His muscles burned. The whole left side of his body was in agony as he pushed himself shakily to all four paws.

"What did I say?" Hailstorm's triumphant voice rang through the air. "Predictable."

Typhoon growled. He turned to see Hailstorm and half a dozen others leave the trees. His gaze swept the lineup. None of them were the shifters who had been at the clinic earlier. Not that it mattered. He growled again as he focused on Hailstorm. The rage he'd felt, seeing the other shifter attacking Mia when her back was turned, rose up in his chest again.

He charged. All the others attacked at the same time, and he found himself in the middle of a snapping, growling mob. He batted two away and launched himself at Hailstorm.

In true cowardly fashion, Hailstorm slipped away, allowing two of his men to take the attack. Typhoon sank his teeth into one of their shoulders and hurled the shifter behind him. He turned to snap at another who was coming at him from behind. His claws tore across the face of a third, and he let out a furious snarl that had three of them flinching back.

Typhoon grabbed the scruff of another shifter and twisted hard. The shifter let out a pained yelp as something snapped, and Typhoon released him. The shifter scrambled away from the fight, limping on three legs. The others regrouped, and Typhoon took the opportunity to go at Hailstorm again.

Hailstorm threw himself at a car that Typhoon hadn't seen with a howl. He shifted back to human form and reached for something inside it. Just as Typhoon landed on him, teeth clenched around his leg, Hailstorm whipped around.

A gun gleamed in his hand. Typhoon released his leg and reached for the gun, but was too late. The report of a gunshot echoed off the trees, and a fiery, burning pain hit Typhoon in the pit of his stomach.

Coward.

Typhoon's teeth clamped over Hailstorm's arm. He shook himself hard. A cold feeling seeped around the burn in his stomach, cutting off the pain.

Hailstorm let out a cry. His arm snapped, and the gun fell to the ground. Typhoon dragged him away from the weapon. The cold feeling spread through his body, and he found himself panting for breath. Hot blood dripped from his belly, and his head spun.

He needed something. He needed...blood.

A whine erupted from Typhoon's throat when two of the other shifters attacked him from behind. Teeth and claws tore into his flanks, the pain muted by the cold seeping through his body. Typhoon knew the signs. He stumbled, fighting the cold, the pain, everything. The growing need for blood rose like flames in the back of his throat. He turned sharply to snap at the two, but they jumped out of range from his teeth.

His wolf had begun to withdraw. Typhoon desperately clung to it, trying to coax it back to the forefront, but it slipped away like water, and he hit the ground on his hands and knees, fingers digging into the gravel road.

Hailstorm laughed. Fangs erupted from Typhoon's jaws. He let out a howl of anger and despair and threw himself at Hailstorm. The need for blood blinded everything else, and he slammed Hailstorm back to the ground. He heard his enemy's blood pulsing just below the surface, and his gaze narrowed in on Hailstorm's neck.

His enemy let out a strangled shout, fear and shock mixed in his voice. Typhoon dropped his head, and his fangs pierced Hailstorm's throat. Hot blood gushed into his mouth, and Typhoon drank greedily. Warmth rushed through his body as he drank, the pain coming back full-force but accompanied by the itch that told him that his wounds were closing, faster than a shifter's should.

There were cries behind him. Hailstorm clawed at him, struggling hard. Typhoon clutched at him tighter, needing more blood.

Something heavy broke across his back, and Typhoon ripped away, turning to the attacker with a snarl. The others stared at him, eyes wide and terrified. That was when he realized what they were seeing: blood-red eyes, skin too pale to be human, and the scent of rotten fruit mingled with his wild scent. They stared at him with horror, seeing him for what he was—the vampire inside of him.

Typhoon's stomach cramped. His muscles bunched, the desire to attack and the need to run warring inside him. Hailstorm whimpered and whined behind him, and Typhoon remembered: he couldn't let these men go, just like that. Even if they hadn't seen his transformation, they'd still attacked him. Had tried to kill him.

He launched himself at the nearest one, but his feet caught on each other, still weak from his injuries. He managed to catch the enemy around the neck with his hands, but his wolf stayed stubbornly distant. The other shifters let out howls and launched at him simultaneously. Teeth and claws tore into him. What little warmth he'd gotten from drinking from Hailstorm quickly fled as the blood spurted from his body. Pain lanced through him, and he swung blindly, but his movements were too slow, too sluggish, and he couldn't hit even one of his attackers. Darkness faded in and out of his vision.

Teeth sank into his shoulder, and Typhoon let out another howl. He punched the wolf in the ribs, and then all he could do was curl up into a ball. He wrapped his arms around the back of his neck while protecting his throat and stomach with his legs, but it didn't stop his attackers, who tore into him with renewed frenzy. The air was full of snarls and growls as chunks of flesh were torn from his body.

Then there was a yelp as one of his attackers was yanked away. Something thudded heavy against the ground. Another yelp rang through the air followed by another and then another, and the gun went off again. Typhoon flinched, but there was no new pain. The scent of rotten fruit overpowered him as long howls, and yelps faded into the space around him.

Typhoon stayed where he was, curled in a ball. He panted for breath. His body felt utterly frozen. He couldn't have uncurled, even if he wanted to, as he was unable to command his limbs to move. Everything seemed to fade in circles around him, and he let out a groan as his stomach clenched and threatened to rebel.

Hands clasped his arms and pulled them away from his body. This time, Typhoon tried to resist, but he had no strength. His head lolled back. Sunlight streamed into his eyes, making them water, and then he saw a familiar face.

"Hold on, Robby," his father breathed, picking him up. He stumbled a little, but Typhoon had no strength to help him. "Just hold on."

Chapter Nine

Mia

Taking care of her injuries wasn't exactly easy as they were on her back, but they weren't deep. Mia elected to sit in the shower until they stopped bleeding, which only took about ten minutes. Then, since Jasper was in need of a change, she brought him into the shower with her and gently cleaned him while trying not to think about Typhoon.

Once the water started to run cold, she got out and carefully dressed before settling Jasper back into his car seat and cleaning the clinic. When she was done, she was too tired to think about driving, and she curled up in her office—she'd slept over there often enough that she'd decided to put a pull-out couch in there—and tried to sleep, which was difficult, as thoughts of Typhoon kept invading her mind.

He'd never looked so angry before. If he had, the anger hadn't been directed at her. What was going through his mind at that moment? He'd said he didn't want a child, yet he'd bought her at the auction and married her, knowing she had an infant son all the while.

She knew he hadn't intended to stay married to her, and that he was just being a gentleman. If he decided he would stay married to her, was it because they had a child?

Mia didn't want that, as strange as it was. Sure, a man marrying her because he wanted a regular sex buddy was fine, but to do it because he felt obligated? No. No way.

He wouldn't do that, anyway. He'd said it himself—he wasn't interested in being a father. No, he was probably off to figure out how to annul their marriage. Or—she shuddered—he'd decided to deal with Blake. She didn't envy the other shifter, but he *had* attacked both her *and* Typhoon. She understood where the justice came in.

There was a bang outside the office, and Mia bolted upright. As she headed for the door—glancing at Jasper quickly, who, unlike her, was sound asleep—it burst open. The scent of blood and rotten fruit assaulted her nostrils, and she instinctively withdrew.

The vampire standing in the doorway wasn't as pale as they normally were. For him to be out in the sunlight like that he must've drunk shifter blood...and recently. Mia looked at his blood-smeared body, catching the faint, wild scent of him.

She drew back from the vampire, and her tiger rushed to the surface. If he thought she'd go down without a fight, he had another thing coming!

"Mia Efron?" the vampire asked, dark eyes sharp on her face.

"What the hell do you want?"

The vampire stepped forward. "I need you. *Robby* needs you. I've put him in that room. Please, I know you don't have any reason to trust a vampire, but I'm here for your help. Please."

Mia hesitated. Maybe the vampire was genuine. Then again, maybe he wasn't. Could she risk it? Claws grew from her nails. Her teeth sharped in her mouth. Fire-orange fur began to sprout on her body.

"I don't help vampires," she spat at him. "Get out of my clinic or—"

Typhoon's voice came from somewhere behind the vampire. "Mia?"

A ripple of shock went through her. She stood rooted to the spot for a moment before hesitantly stepping forward. "Why would a vampire want to help his greatest enemy?"

The vampire's jaw tightened, and he stepped back as well, though whether to keep drawing Mia forward or to put some distance between them if she decided to attack, she didn't know. The vampire shook his head. "Robby isn't my enemy."

Robby. Mia hesitated a moment longer before shaking her head. She never knew Typhoon's real name; Robby didn't seem to suit him at all. If it really was him...

Some vampires could change their voices, but their vampiric powers lessened substantially after drinking shifter blood. It was mid-day outside—any vampire around there on that day had to have drunk a significant amount of shifter blood, which meant they would no longer have their creepy powers.

"What happened?" she snapped as she swept past the vampire to the room Typhoon was in, pulling up short as soon as she entered.

Typhoon was on the bed, all right, but he didn't look...like himself. His skin was marble-white—his usual tone was closer to a tanned deer hide. Blood red eyes shone from his face, and a set of distinctive fangs was in his mouth. The teeth weren't the curved, pointed fangs of a shifter, either. These were straight, sharpened on both sides, and distinctly vampiric.

Horror flooded her chest as she backed up a step. Shifters couldn't be turned into vampires. They were poisoned by the venom. The result of the vampire DNA trying to rewrite the shifter DNA was always fatal.

She'd seen Typhoon shift into his wolf; it was impossible for him to be a vampire! *Impossible*!

"Is this some sort of joke?" she rasped.

Typhoon's gaze was wide and terrified as it locked on her. He panted heavily and tried to push himself up, but his body was so battered, it was a miracle he was even conscious. His gaze flickered to the vampire. “Why bring me—” His eyes rolled into the back of his head, and he went limp. Blood dripped from his hands to the floor.

The vampire rushed to his side and cradled him gently. His dark eyes turned pleadingly to Mia. “Please, he needs blood. I didn’t know where else to take him.”

“Blood?” Mia’s brain didn’t seem to want to work. What the hell was going on? What was happening? “Because...he’s a vampire?”

“Only half. Please, I can explain once he’s healed. You have blood here, don’t you? This is a clinic where you treat injured shifters—you have to have blood."

"We suffered some bad attacks lately," Mia murmured. "I haven't had time to replenish my stores."

The last of it had been taken by the human paramedics when they'd transported the patients to the hospital. There was no blood left in the clinic except for vampire blood. She opened her mouth to say that she did have blood, after all, when the vampire hissed under his breath.

"You'll have to feed him, then. I can't. My blood will only make it worse."

Mia felt paralyzed as she stared at Typhoon's face. He was getting weaker by the second, the smell of rotting fruit growing stronger. The scent of blood was almost overpowering even though the flow from his wounds had begun to slow. What would happen when he ran out of blood entirely? Would he die, or would he just be vampire through and through?

The vampire stroked his hair, and tears leaked from his eyes. The sight of him crying and the gentle way he held onto Typhoon triggered something in Mia's brain. She couldn't just sit there and do nothing while a *vampire* took care of someone in need of help.

Mia strode forward and yanked her sleeve up her arm. It crossed her mind that if anybody else had still been at the clinic, Typhoon and the vampire would have both been dead by then, and there was nothing she could have done to stop it. Her stomach cramped, but she pushed the thoughts aside. There wasn't anybody else there besides her, the vampire, Typhoon…and Jasper.

Oh, Goddess! If Typhoon was a vampire, what did that make Jasper?

"What do I need to do?" Mia asked, holding her wrist over Typhoon's face—she wasn't putting her neck anywhere near those fangs.

"Just put your wrist in his mouth. Instinct will take over."

Typhoon tensed. His eyes flickered, and he let out a protesting noise. "Don't…hurt…"

The vampire stroked his hair again. "I won't let that happen, Robby. I promise. I won't let you hurt her. I'll make sure you stop."

Typhoon groaned. His head flopped to one side. How much time was left?

The vampire pinned Typhoon to the table, and Mia took a deep breath. Without allowing herself to think of anything else, she pressed her wrist into Typhoon's mouth.

Typhoon whimpered. His eyes flashed open. His bloody irises locked on her, and his jaw opened. Typhoon bit down on Mia's wrist so fast and hard that she could do nothing else but jerk, and a cry of pain burst forth from her lips.

Typhoon's teeth tore through her skin, and he began to suck. Pain lanced up her arm, starting at where his mouth connected with her. Dark growls rolled from his chest.

Mia yanked away instinctively, and Typhoon snarled as he lunged.

“Don’t stop him," the vampire gasped, "not yet.” He struggled to hold Typhoon in place.

Blood dripped from Mia's wrist, but she put her arm back against Typhoon’s mouth, nevertheless, and he began to suck again. She could feel the blood leaving her body. Soon, her legs became shaky.

“I can’t,” she stuttered.

Her knee buckled, and she leaned against the table, gasping for breath. She wanted to pull away again, but Typhoon’s struggles had grown stronger, and she didn’t dare. What if he broke free and went for her throat?

The vampire wrapped his arms around Typhoon's body, climbed onto the table, and pinned him into place. Go," he grunted. "Quickly!"

Mia's brain started to spin. At first, she wasn't certain what the vampire was saying.

"*Go*!"

Her tiger yowled, and instinct took over as Mia ripped herself away from Typhoon. She stumbled toward the door, hearing curses and screams rise up behind her.

The vampire grunted with the effort of keeping Typhoon pinned. The noise had obviously woken Jasper because a thin wail came from her office. Mia raced to her son, snatching up the car seat on the way. Her keys sat on her desk, and she almost missed them as she went for the door. Mia's legs shook, and her arms felt heavy. She could hardly keep herself upright as she swayed toward the building entrance.

A howl broke from behind her, and she put on as much speed as she could. She raced to her car, hurriedly clicked the car seat into place, and jumped into the driver’s seat. Mia had to get away from there, just go as far as she could.

Typhoon was...what? A vampire, a shifter, or somehow both? She’d heard rumors that some vampires were looking to create vampire-shifter hybrids, but that was new. Typhoon was at least thirty-five years old, a little older than she was. If there'd been a vampire-shifter hybrid running around for thirty-plus years, she'd have known about it, right?

And he was always the last person to show mercy to vampires. If he was a vampire himself, why would he do that? Unless, of course, he was working from this side to weaken the Brotherhood to bring them to a point where an all-out war was necessary.

Was Jasper the vampire-shifter hybrid they wanted? What would happen to him if the Brotherhood found out? Would their protective feelings for her be enough to save him?

"Goddesses of old and new, protect us," she whispered, terror slithering through her blood. If such goddesses existed, would they care about one insignificant tiger?

She didn't know where she was going until she ended up outside of a familiar mansion. It wasn't as big as his one in Ivywood, but Josef had a house in every city in which the Brotherhood had a chapter, Easthallow included.

Mia wrapped a strip of cloth around her wrist as she pulled up to the gate.

A bored-sounding voice came from the speaker at the side of the driveway. “Name and business.”

“Mia Efron.” Should she tell them what happened or pretend she was checking up on Andy? Maybe neither. “I need to come in, please. Roxy and Josef know me.”

There was a brief pause before the gates swung inward. Mia let out a relieved sigh as she drove in.

Roxy and Josef were waiting for her at the front door, both of them looking confused and concerned. Mia no longer wanted to talk about anything she'd witnessed as she got out of her car. Jasper fussed, and exhaustion took over.

“Is everything okay?” Roxy asked, coming down to greet her.

Mia stared past her and shook her head. “I need a place to stay for a while. Somewhere safe.”

“Safe from what?” Josef pressed.

Bile rose in Mia’s throat. “Just safe. Please, can I stay here?”

Roxy put an arm around her. “Of course. Do you have any bags?”

“No.” She had even taken a diaper bag. She swayed on the spot, and her chin fell to her chest. “I need to rest.”

“Of course. I’ll show you to a room.”

***

Mia decided not to tell Roxy and Josef anything. Instead, she slept for as long as she could, before getting up to search for Roxy. She found her sitting with her little girl and Jasper. Roxy looked concerned, but she didn't press when Mia said she didn't want to talk about it. The tiger curled up on the couch, feeling utterly exhausted despite her sleep. It was impossible to know how much blood she'd lost, but that wasn't the point.

Just as Roxy had opened her mouth, Mia's phone rang. She flinched at the sound since it had heralded nothing but intense work, exhaustion, and confusion these past few days. When Mia checked it, she saw that it was Typhoon calling her. The air whooshed from her lungs, and she stared uncertainly at the phone.

"Did Typhoon do something?" Roxy asked, glaring at the phone.

Mia stood. "I don't know. I...I have to take this."

She hurriedly left the room, knowing that Roxy's sharp ears would pick up the conversation even if Mia wore earbuds. She managed to answer just before it went to voicemail, and took a deep breath before putting the phone to her ear.

"Hello?"

"Hey." Typhoon sounded cautious and uncertain. "I wasn't sure you'd answer."

"I wasn't sure either."

There was a beat of silence. “Can we talk? In person? There’s just a lot…I don’t think going over it all on the phone is going to really work.”

He had a point there. There was no telling who might hear the conversation while they were on the phone. Besides that, she needed to see his face to know if he was telling the truth. In any case, she needed answers. Even if the thought of going to Typhoon and finding out he was in league with the vampires was terrifying, she needed answers. Not just to know what he was, but for Jasper. She had a responsibility to her son, and she had to know if she was going to handle this properly.

“We can meet,” she said slowly. “I’ll see you back at the clinic.”

"Thank you," Typhoon breathed, and then he hung up.

Chapter Ten

Typhoon

What was worse: ending up in a state where he could hurt Mia while she tried to help him, or relying on his father for protection? He didn't remember much about drinking from her, only the hot blood on his tongue and the desperation to stop but the inability to do so. Typhoon had never before been at a point where he'd been too injured to control the vampire urges.

"Is it always like that?" he rasped.

His father stood nearby, staring at a blank wall while emotion warred on his face. "No. That was an extreme reaction."

Typhoon turned his face away, ashamed of his entire existence. What right did he have to live if he would one day end up like his father, killing the people closest to him?

"It's not your fault, Robby. You've never gone into bloodlust before. There are always measures that can be taken to prevent it in the future. I'm certain your mate will understand."

But Mia wasn't his mate, was she? They'd been brought together through a series of random circumstances and nothing more. And yet the memory of her turning away from him made his stomach cramp. Maybe it was because out of everyone he knew, she was the only one with whom he could relax. She was the only person he knew for certain wouldn't turn around and stab him in the back. He knew that if Mia rejected him, there was nobody left to accept him.

Well, maybe not nobody. He snuck a look at his father whose face was still blank. “How did you know where to find me?”

“I didn’t. I heard a commotion and decided to check it out. When I saw those men beating on you…” Anger flashed over his father’s face. “Vampires aren’t the only ones who suffer from bloodlust.”

“It’s not the same.” Typhoon glanced away. Shifters had their berserkers, people who ended up so deep in fighting mode, they could turn against their own mates. Thunder’s sister, Shadow, had seen such a condition, but nobody ever said she should be put down over it. “It’s not the same.”

His father turned to him, face resolute but also full of grief. “I know that it’s different for you, but you have to know, Robby: I love you. I will always be here for you, no matter what. Even if you can never forgive me, I understand, and I will be here whenever you need me.”

Typhoon shook his head. This time he didn’t correct his father when he called him by the wrong name. His heart clenched when he thought about what it must have been like for him to awake from his hunger for blood to find the woman he loved, dead by his own hand.

“Did you love her?” Typhoon asked hoarsely.

His father didn’t hesitate to answer. “With all my heart. If it weren't for you, knowing I had to look after you the best I could, I would have ended myself after her death. Every day I think—"

"She loved you." Typhoon blinked back tears.

"I know. I wish she hadn't. Maybe then…"

A car pulled into the clinic's parking lot. It was Mia. Typhoon took a deep breath, trying to calm the clenching in his stomach. She got out of the car looking grim and determined, and Typhoon got to his feet. He'd never spent much time in waiting rooms before, but this past hour was almost more than he could take. He briefly wondered if she'd brought Jasper with her but dismissed it. She wouldn't bring her baby into a situation where he might end up hurt.

Mia marched into the clinic and stood by the door, her gaze sweeping from him to his father. Her jaw tightened, and he saw the faintest of stripes appearing on her skin; she was keeping her tiger close to the surface. For a moment, Typhoon was disappointed she'd come to the meeting expecting the worst, but he really couldn't blame her. How was she supposed to trust them when it came to vampires?

Typhoon turned to his father. "You should probably leave. Give the two of us a chance to talk on our own. Just stay out of sight and don't go too far. If anybody finds you here—"

"I know. I am well aware of the Brotherhood's policies toward vampires." There was no condemnation in his voice, but Typhoon flinched anyway.

He wished Twister had been right, and not for the first time. If there was another way, then perhaps things could be better for everybody, but there wasn't another way, was there? There were just too many vampires who didn't want change. Those that did were just as likely to be murdered by the Brotherhood as they were by the zealots in their covens and kingdoms.

The status quo was the status quo for a reason.

Mia edged backward as Typhoon's father headed for the door. He paused to look at her before glancing back at Typhoon and sighing.

"You should know that he didn't want to come here. He would have rather died than put you and your son in danger."

Mia flinched, but she didn't speak until the vampire was gone. When she did, she turned an accusing glare on Typhoon. "So, who exactly was that, and why does he care about you?"

Now, it was Typhoon's turn to flinch. He ran a hand through his hair and shook his head. There was no easy way to say it. Any of it. "He's my father."

Disbelief colored her face.

"I know what it sounds like," he hurried to say, "but it's true: he's my father. I'm a shifter, but I also have...vampire in me. I'm a hybrid. It's why I'm...the way I am. Bigger. Stronger. I know it sounds impossible, but—"

“There have been attempts to create vampire-shifter hybrids in the past. So what? You’re the result of some sort of...experiment?” Mia folded her arms over her chest and glared at him.

“No, it's not like that.” His shoulders sagged and he slumped into a chair. He felt so very tired—who wouldn't after being beaten to within an inch of his life, his vampire side bursting out in full bloodlust, and all the time it took for him to heal. His gut still ached, even if he had healed faster than any regular shifter could. “My parents didn’t mean to have me. They didn’t know it could happen.”

“Then what happened? How were you born?”

Typhoon rubbed his neck. “My mother met my father when she was quite young. Something crazy, like eighteen. She used to say that she knew he was the one for her the moment she laid eyes on him. She chased him for years, apparently, while he tried to discourage her attention. Eventually, she ended up witnessing the Brotherhood attacking his coven. He managed to escape, and she hid him. Fed him her blood, though they were careful that he never actually bit her. She fell deeper in love and eventually, he returned the feelings."

Mia inched forward, hesitant belief warring with distrust on her face. "And since she was feeding him her blood, he was more human than he otherwise would have been, allowing him to get her pregnant."

"Yeah."

“And then what?”

“Mom never talked about those times. She said that her pregnancy accelerated faster than was normal—she was full-term in something like a month. Then I was born.

"The vampire in me was clear.

"My father took off. He couldn’t be with us, not when the Brotherhood was around. The few visits he made while growing up put us in danger. At least, that’s what he claimed. I know the Brotherhood would have killed all of us if they found us, but why stay in a city run by the Brotherhood if that was the case?”

They both fell silent for a moment. Typhoon stared ahead, watching the sun dance patterns in the shadows coming through the tree leaves outside. There wasn't much else he could tell her about the history between her parents. Well, there *was* the big part. He sucked in a deep breath, preparing to tell her about how his mother had died.

"Your mother's pregnancy only lasted a month, right?"

"Yeah."

"So...how long did it take for you to grow to maturity?"

Typhoon shifted, suddenly embarrassed. "Uh...well, it was only a year."

Mia turned disbelieving eyes on him. "So you're what—ten years old?"

Her tone, disgusted, brought his hackles up. "My chronological age is irrelevant. I am a full adult, both mentally and physically. I have been since I was one year old," he added, hoping to lighten the mood a little. It fell flat, so he pushed ahead. "If I wasn't, I wouldn't be able to leave the Savage Brotherhood."

She didn't look uncertain, but she nodded slowly. Mia would accept it—at least for now.

"My mother—"

"When you drank my blood, you didn't poison me." She clasped her hands over her knees. Her gaze was steely.

Typhoon hesitated a moment before nodding at her to continue. If she wanted to control how the conversation, he wasn't going to stop her. Not in this case, at least. He needed her to stay and listen to him until he'd convinced her to keep his secret. If he pushed, she was bound to leave, and he'd have lost his chance. He'd have to go on the run, just to survive. Finding a place where the Savage Brotherhood didn't yet have a chapter wasn't likely to be enough, either.

He'd be hunted down.

"So, even with your…full vampire side coming out, you don't have any venom?"

Typhoon shook his head. "No. I think it's because I'm a hybrid. I guess you could say I'm sterile—at least, the vampire side of me is."

"Is that normal?" Her voice pitched, her eyes grew brighter, and her hands clasped tighter.

Ah. So they were getting to the part with which she was most concerned. "I don't know. I'm the only hybrid I know of."

"So, you don't have any siblings?"

"No. My mother...she died when I was in the equivalence of my teens."

Mia stared at him for a moment before she nodded. Her shoulders hitched as she took in a deep breath. Deeper than necessary, really. "So, what does that mean for Jasper?"

Typhoon wanted to reassure her. He wanted to tell her everything was going to be fine and that she didn't have anything to worry about. He wanted that fear in her eyes to disperse. He wanted her to smile at him again. He wanted her to be the self-assured, strong, stubborn woman he knew. He wanted to pull her into his arms and whisper that nothing was ever going to harm her baby—not as long as he was around.

He wasn't even certain where the desires had come from. Surely, it didn't make that much of a difference to him whether she trusted him or not.

"I don't know. Like I said, I'm the only one I know of. Was your pregnancy normal?"

Mia frowned at him, then shrugged. "Mostly, yeah. He was preterm. And he's very small, even for his age. He's more developed in other ways, though. He seems...smarter. It's not like he's crawling or anything yet, but he does seem to be developing mentally much quicker than the average shifter-child."

Typhoon nodded. "But he's not growing faster?"

“Not that I've noticed.”

“Good.” He leaned back and let out a deep sigh. “Maybe, since you’re a shifter and the vampire part of me is so repressed...Are there tests we can do? To see how much of *that* part he inherited? Maybe see if he inherited it at all?”

Mia shrugged. “Maybe. I haven’t had a lot of time to wrap my head around it, so I can’t say for certain.

"What happened to you not wanting to be a father?”

“It’s a little late for that, isn’t it?’ Typhoon hid his face in his hands for a moment, struggling to put his thoughts in order. “I’ve always been cautious. I never wanted this...whatever I am to be passed on to a child. I never thought it would be fair to them, and quite frankly, I don’t know if I ever had the chance to decide for myself if I even wanted to be a father, but the fact is: Jasper is mine...if you're certain?"

He looked up at her hopefully. Maybe she'd take it back.

Mia stared at him, trembling. She nodded. "You're the only one who could be his father, but that doesn't make him yours."

Typhoon took a moment to accept that before continuing. "I *am* his father, and that means he may have inherited parts of me. I can't just ignore that, but I also won't force my presence on you if you don't want me around. I just...I just ask that you not tell anybody, because if they knew—"

"If they knew, Jasper's life would be in danger." Mia's eyes flashed as she stood. "I'm not letting anything happen to my son, Typhoon...or should I start calling you Robby?"

He blinked in surprise. The words and the tone just didn't match up. He opened his mouth, closed it, then shook his head. "My name's Typhoon. My mother used to call me Robby, but I haven't been him for a long time." He took a moment to study her. She'd begun to relax, which he took as a hopeful sign. "That leaves us," he said. It was, of course, the most difficult part of the conversation.

"Us," Mia repeated.

"Yeah, us."

"*Is* there an us?"

Typhoon shrugged. "Well, we *are* married. We do have a kid together. As crazy as all this is, it's something we have to figure out, isn't it?"

"Is it?" Mia's gaze closed off. "Or is it one of those things that would be better off ignored?

"We had sex. I got pregnant. We got married because you were worried I'd been forced into the auction. Now we have this huge secret that could potentially ruin both of our lives. If you think we have to be together—"

"Of course, I don't think we *have* to be together."

"Then what are you—"

The door opened, making them both jump. Typhoon turned and opened his mouth to yell at whomever it was, but his voice died on his tongue. Blake was standing there, his gun buried in

Typhoon’s father’s side. There was a bandage taped to Blake’s neck. He sneered, and he jabbed the gun deeper into his father's side.

“Tell me, Typhoon: why would a vampire help out the Savage Brotherhood's alpha?”

Typhoon snarled, his muscles tense.

Blake stared at him, hard fury in his eyes. “What are you, and what do you want from us?”

Chapter Eleven

Mia

As if the situation wasn't bad enough.

Mia tensed, backing up a little from Blake and the vampire. While Blake looked almost unhinged, halfway between gleeful and hateful, the vampire was tense, his eyes locked on Typhoon as though trying to tell him something. What that was, Mia had no idea.

A good ten men filed into the clinic behind Blake. Mia was very aware that it was just her and Typhoon there, alone. They'd been so engrossed in their conversation, they hadn't noticed the guys until it was too late. If it came to a fight, would she be a target? Blake had a gun, for that matter; a *gun!* What sort of shifter brought a weapon to a fight when he had perfectly good claws?

A shifter who doesn't think he'll win any other way.

Mia opened her mouth to demand that Blake and his cronies leave, but as she did, Blake's gaze shot to her.

"And you: harboring a vampire, are we? What other secrets do you hold? How will the others react once they hear about this? How many of them will jump to your defense then?"

Maybe it would be better for her—and for Jasper—if she just fell back and didn't get involved. Her heart beat rapidly. How could she do that, though? She was a doctor. She'd sworn an oath to save lives. If she turned her back on that oath, how could she keep practicing, even if was to save her own skin?

You wanted to quit, a small voice whispered in the back of her head.

But she didn't, she told it. She just wanted to take care of her son.

Typhoon shifted positions, placing himself in front of her. He lifted his hands toward Blake as though trying to placate him, but it didn't work. Blake tensed even more, and Typhoon's father hissed as though he was suddenly in pain. He shook his head rapidly. Blake prodded him with the gun, and he was still again. There were fury and determination in his eyes that made him look more like Typhoon's smaller brother.

"That vampire," Typhoon said slowly, "is an informant of mine. He has been keeping an eye on Cromwell for me and has provided the Brotherhood with a lot of necessary information that—"

"Liar!"

Blake shoved Typhoon's father across the floor. He stumbled into Typhoon, and the shifter quickly steadied him and pushed him back. Typhoon stood there, protecting both Mia and his father from Blake. She clenched her hands. There had to be something she could do, right? If they could only stop this from turning into a fight...

It didn't seem like Blake was interested in settling the matter peacefully, though. He lifted the gun and pointed it at Typhoon's head. "You have been getting soft. Everybody knows it. Twister's only the last in the long line.

"And I saw your eyes when you attacked me. I felt you *drinking my blood*. So, what are you: a vampire lover or a vampire yourself?"

Typhoon was silent for a long moment. What was he supposed to say to that?

Mia found herself stepping forward. She clenched her hands as she stepped up beside Typhoon. Maybe all of it was crazy, and it was all happening too fast, but she wasn't about to just give up on it. Her mouth felt dry, but she gathered her courage, mustered all the authority she had, and put her hands on her hips. Several of the shifters behind Blake glanced at her nervously. Stephen was there, looking like he wanted to tell her to stay out of it.

“We don’t know what happened with Typhoon,” she said, trying to infuse her voice with confidence despite her words. “He came to me after you attacked him, and he drank your blood—”

Please let that be what happened, she prayed.

“And we were about to start some tests to see what was going on. As you know, Typhoon has been bitten and infected by vampires many times.”

He'd never been bitten. At the very least, he'd never been infected. Was he, as a half-vampire, immune to their venom?

“I suspect that might be a contributing factor. I don’t appreciate you coming into my clinic and waving a gun around like a barbarian. We're dealing with the situation, so please, leave."

Blake turned to her just as she was finishing her spiel. He glared at her for a long moment before something sparked in his eyes. Blake shook his head, though he kept the gun pointed at Typhoon.

"I don't want to see you get hurt, Mia. I'm sorry for what I did before—I lost my head—but I'm not leaving while this... *creature* and his pet vampire are on the loose. You need to leave now, before things get bloody."

"If you think I'm going to just walk away and let you kill people, you've got another thing coming."

The muscles in Blake's jaw worked. "You're a doctor, not a fighter."

“Yeah, I am a doctor, which means I know anatomy. I also know how to fight. I’m a doctor who is consistently in the line of danger because of who I treat. If you try anything, I know how to take you down. And if you hurt my mate, my...husband,” she quickly corrected, heat rising in her cheeks (even that seemed too...intimate a term), “then believe me when I say that you'll regret it. The next time you need my skills...”

She trailed off, letting the threat hang.

“Leave, Mia,” Blake said again. His eyes narrowed, and a growl filled his voice. “You don’t know the danger this thing poses for you.”

“Typhoon's not a—"

“Mia.” Typhoon interrupted. He turned slightly, his gaze capturing hers. “You need to leave.”

She gaped at him.

“I don’t want you here,” he continued. “Blake, here, is clearly out for blood, and I don’t want yours to end up being spilled. You could easily get caught in the crossfire, and your son needs you, not mine.” Typhoon glared at Blake. “He’s not my son; he’s half-human.”

Was that his way of trying to protect Jasper when his own heritage came out? Mia didn’t speak; she didn't know what to say.

Typhoon’s father shifted behind them. Mia glanced back to see a torn expression on his face, and she wondered if he was deciding if he should chance running? Or...she thought about how she'd feel if it was Jasper instead of Typhoon beside her, and she was the one standing at the back of the room, her son in danger because of her presence. She'd be torn between wanting to divorce herself from him—for his sake—and wanting to launch herself at the people threatening him.

And that must have been exactly what Typhoon's father was feeling.

She swallowed hard and looked back at Typhoon. "Look...I didn't want you to have vampires as informants. I said you couldn't trust them, and I hold to that, though there are some decent vamps out there, like Queen Guinevere. If it weren't for her, we'd have lost a lot of men," here, she turned to glare at Stephen, "you, included."

He shifted from foot to foot, ducking his head.

Mia glanced back at Typhoon. “I’m not going anywhere. I have to stand for what I think is right, and right now...” She narrowed her eyes at Blake. “Right now, that means helping you take this punk down. But I do ask that you try not to kill him.”

“Dammit, Mia!” Typhoon moved, as though trying to shield her while Blake growled. “Don’t you see what’s happening here? Someone's about to die here, and I won’t let it be you!”

“And I won’t let it be you!” She whirled on him, putting her back to Blake even though her tiger snarled and clawed at her chest, telling her she was an idiot for doing it. “You are the most boar-headed, stupid, stubborn man I've ever known, but if I walk away and let you die without trying to stop it I'd never forgive myself...I love you."

Typhoon's eyes widened.

Mia laughed at her own dramatic confession. What a time to say it. What a time for her to realize it. Tears blurred her eyes. Her heart clenched at the thought of anything happening to him. "Fuck you. I never wanted to fall in love. Fuck you and your smile and your voice and the way you never let anybody see your soft side! Fuck you for showing me parts of you that made me fall in love with you! *Fuck you*!"

There were some murmurs and whispers from Blake's men. Typhoon's father stared with a slack jaw from behind them, but Mia didn't look at any of them. She didn't care about any of them. Her heart beat shallowly, her confession hanging between them as though it were a tangible thing, as though telling Typhoon she loved him would stop Blake from shooting them both.

"Mia..." Typhoon reached out. He touched her cheek and grasped both of her shoulders. "You are one crazy cat."

He lifted her, even as she hissed in anger. Her hiss became a shriek as he threw her in the air, and she skidded over the top of the receptionist's desk and fell heavily behind it.

The gun went off. The crack of the shot echoed around her, making her stomach clench. There was a grunt followed by a cry.

The gun went off again. This time, the bullet hit the wall, just over her head. She threw herself sideways and out from behind the desk.

Typhoon and Blake wrestled, the gun clasped in both of their hands while Blake’s men fanned out. Several of them went for Typhoon’s father while a few of them jumped in and beat on Typhoon.

A snarl rose from her chest. This wasn’t happening—not if she had anything to say about it!

Mia flung herself forward, bringing her tiger forth as she did. Her clothes shredded from her body, and she tackled the two men at once. Both of them cried out as she brought them down. Her claws raked across one of their backs, and she closed her jaws around the other's shoulder and wrenched her body. The shoulder snapped; the shifter gave a cry of pain.

She turned to the other and broke his arm before leaping off and onto the back of one of the shifters attempting to punch Typhoon's father out. The shifter dodged, but he wasn't fast enough to avoid her claws.

Pain spiked through her hindquarters, and Mia whirled, slapping at the wolf who had sunk his teeth into her flank. Her paw hit him with her claws extended, sending a burst of fur into the air. The wolf let go, caterwauling in pain. Mia sprang on one of her back paws as another wolf rushed her, head-on. She came down on its back, clawing along its sides and snapping every inch of his body within reach. It yipped and rolled in an attempt to get away from her.

A bear suddenly appeared in the room and swiped at Typhoon's father.

Mia dodged, seizing it by the armpit, and it turned a huge paw on her. She wasn't able to release it in time, and the blow knocked her over, sending her rolling until she came to a stop near Blake and Typhoon's feet. She took the opportunity to slash at Blake, but he jumped aside.

There were a good four more men who were helping him fight Typhoon. The gun had disappeared; where it was, Mia didn't bother to find out.

She threw herself between Typhoon and two of his attackers, forcing them to retreat and give him some breathing space. His massive fist crashed into one of their faces, and the shifter crumpled to the floor and was still.

The bear went after Typhoon's father again. His father had broken the leg off a chair and was using it to wedge the bear's mouth open, preventing it from biting down on his head. Another shifter came up behind him and punched him in the ribs.

Mia sprang over to them and yanked the feet out from under him with her teeth while clawing at the bear's face. Typhoon's father grunted as he attempted to duck under the bear's paws only to be clipped on the side of the head. He went down, prompting Typhoon to let out a strangled shout.

Blake laughed in triumph. Mia turned to find him holding the gun once more. Three shifters had Typhoon. One of them kicked his feet out from under him as Blake aimed the gun at Typhoon.

Stephen lunged from the side, knocking Blake over. The gun went off, the bullet flying wildly. Mia sprang onto the bear's back, tearing its neck as it turned while Blake and Stephen wrestled on the ground and Typhoon managed to throw off the shifters holding him.

The bear roared as Mia hit a nerve through its thick hide, causing its whole body to shudder.

Blake elbowed Stephen in the face and went for the gun.

Typhoon lunged.

There was a crack.

The bear threw Mia off, and she hit the wall hard. Several cries rang out and then there was silence. Typhoon's father panted for breath. He was sitting at an awkward angle, clutching his leg.

Mia scrambled to her feet and shifted back into her human form once the fighting had ceased. Everybody turned to stare at Blake's limp body.

Typhoon panted for breath as he leaned against the wall, lifting his dark gaze to glare at his would-be attackers. "I don't want any more death here," he growled. "And you can be assured the human police have been called. Get out now, and I might give you a chance to run."

There was a moment of stillness before the vast majority of shifters dashed for the entrance. They helped those who couldn't walk, but they left Stephen and a couple others behind. It wasn't until Typhoon helped them stand that Mia realized that the ones left must have turned to help him.

“The police will be on their way, won’t they? That busybody next door would've called them.” Mia looked around the bloody, ruined waiting room and shook her head. “They’re going to shut me down.”

“You wanted to quit anyway.” Typhoon walked over to his father and lifted him into a chair.

Mia couldn’t argue with that. She went over to check on his father and grimaced to see the leg had been broken so badly.

“I’ll be fine,” he rasped, sweat dewing on his brow.

“I should still splint that. You’re awfully human right now.”

Typhoon's father grimaced.

Typhoon stood and headed into the back. He returned a little later with a set of scrubs and thrust them at Mia's chest without looking at her. "We need to get our story straight."

She took the clothes, her heart sinking. Even after she dressed, Typhoon wouldn't look at her. Her confession from before the fight seemed to hang in the air, and she could almost kick herself because of it. What had she been thinking, telling him that? The only thing he wanted less than a child was a mate to tie him down.

Maybe they should've had the "us" talk, she thought bitterly as she took care of the injured few left behind. Maybe then she wouldn't have been so stupid as to tell him that she loved him, but she would have eventually. And she knew she would have because it was true.

Chapter Twelve

Typhoon

"I never thought I'd would ever do this." Typhoon stood next to his recently-fixed bike, fiddling with the edges of his leather jacket so they'd cover more of his tattoos. He glanced up briefly at his father, then dropped his gaze again.

"I never thought you would, either." His father let out a slow breath and just as slowly, reached across the space between them to put a hand on his shoulder. "I know that my words don't mean anything to you, but I'm proud of you, Robby. I'm proud of the man you've become. Your mother would be proud, too."

Typhoon shook his head. She wouldn't be proud; she'd be hurt that he was so cut off from everything in his life except for violence and the Brotherhood. From that point on, though, he would live a life that she would be proud of. Protecting people but allowing softness and love into his life as well. Allowing forgiveness.

He sucked in a deep breath as he looked up. Guinevere's posse, a collection of hummers and jeeps, was visible down the road. Typhoon didn't have much time to say what he needed to. "It's not your fault."

His father's brow furrowed.

"What happened. Mom. How off the rails I went. It's not your fault." He made his gaze meet his father's. "It's not your fault. It was just...circumstances."

His father's grip tightened. Typhoon could see that he wanted to argue the point, to say that it was his fault, but Typhoon shook his head. They needed to have much more of a talk than could be shared at that moment. Right then, he just wanted a moment where maybe he and his father weren't so very different, after all. The tightness in his chest eased just a little bit, and a weight he hadn't known he was carrying sloughed off his shoulders.

"I love you, Dad," he whispered as Guinevere's cars pulled to a stop next to them.

"I love you, too," his father whispered back.

They stepped away from one another. Guinevere left her car, looking very pixie-like next to the hulking figures cut by her bodyguards. Her gaze swept around and her brow furrowed when she saw it was just the two of them. She strode forward and nodded to Typhoon.

"Alpha. What can I do for you?"

Typhoon gestured to his father. "This vampire was a contact in Cromwell's kingdom, but he was discovered, and I need a safe place for him to go to now."

Guinevere's eyes widened slightly. She inspected his father for a moment before smiling. A true vampire queen, she wasn't about to let an opportunity in which the Savage Brotherhood would owe her a favor go by. "I would be more than happy to take him in, then."

His father nodded his thanks. He got into the hummer with Guinevere and glanced back at Typhoon to give him a small smile. Typhoon returned it, suddenly wishing he'd told his father that he could call anytime. Then again, maybe it had that been implied.

He stood there, watching them go until the posse was out of sight before climbing onto his bike with a sigh. That had been taken care of, but there was so much more to deal with. He already knew that his “decision” to have a vampire contact would have a backlash. How could he show mercy to them without allowing Twister his place among the gang?

He was alpha, and he would weather it. There was something far more important for him to sort out at that point in time.

Mia's clinic had been briefly shut down, due to what had happened there lately, but Hurricane came in with his lawyers and his money and got it open again. Even so, Mia took a few days off to figure out what she wanted. Luck was with her in that there had been no further disasters, meaning she could actually have those days without worrying about stitching people up after another vampire attack.

With that in mind, Typhoon headed for her house. He found her sitting outside on the bench-swing, sleeping baby cradled in her arms, her Kindle in hand. She watched him walk up the path, and a small smile flashed on her face. Mia remained stiff otherwise.

What felt like a ball of snakes fought in his stomach. He envied people who wound up with nothing more than butterflies when facing a nervous situation. He wasn't at all certain how he was meant to go from there. Mia's admission of love rang in his ears with every step he took. He'd thought about it every night since Blake's death. He'd avoided Mia during that time, not wanting her to say that she had just been talking as she tried to put Blake off.

Now that he was there, he had a few things he wanted to say himself.

"Typhoon," she said coolly when he reached her. "I've been trying to call."

"Yeah, I know. I'm sorry. I've needed some time to think."

"You said as much in your text."

"Yeah." Typhoon knelt at her feet. His gaze turned to Jasper. "I've been thinking, and first off, I wanted to tell you that I'm sorry for running away like I did when I found out that Jasper was my son. I don't know how to explain it, other than I was…terrified about what my heritage would mean for him. Not to mention how you'd react once you'd found out about my father."

Mia stroked Jasper's head and sighed. "I can't blame you for that. And it was unexpected, so…thank you for your apology. I want to apologize, too, for not telling you. So that you had to find out with Blake."

"Could've done without that, but I know why you didn't."

Mia nodded, the stiffness of her smile fading a little. She blinked rapidly, and he thought he saw tears on her lashes.

"I want to say something: I know that you want to be free of all of this, free of the danger, free of the uncertainty, free of the Brotherhood and vampires and all the violence, but I'm the alpha. I have a responsibility. I've wanted there to be another way for a long time, and now I'm in a position where I might be able to find another way.

"I can't leave now. I'll be a target as long as I'm alpha, from outside the Brotherhood and within it. If there is an us, you'll never be free of danger."

Mia nodded. "I know."

Typhoon waited for a beat before pulling in a deep breath. "With that in mind, I...I don't know what the future is. I can't promise I'll be able to protect you."

Mia reached out and pressed a finger to his lips. "I'm holding the future."

Once more, his gaze was drawn to the baby.

“Jasper is our future, if, that is, we have a future together. I know there'll be danger, and I can’t promise I’ll always be good with that. I also can’t promise I won’t have doubts when it comes to the Brotherhood, but if you’ll have me, I can promise I'll never have doubts about you and your place in my life and my heart.”

Tears pooled in his eyes at her words, and he wiped them away, embarrassed, but a smile still spread over his face. “I’ll have you. I’ll have you every night if I can. I've had to be alone for a long time, and I thought love was weakness, but I love you. I already love Jasper, as much as being a father terrifies me, so if you’re willing, I’d like to make this real. To be mates for real.”

“Oh, Typhoon, we already are.” She cupped his face and rolled her eyes at him, her face breaking into a wide smile. “When two shifters love each other and are willing to fight for each other, doesn’t that make them mates?”

“Yeah, I guess it does. And…I’d like it if you called me Robby.”

Her smile was like the sun. “I’d like that, too.”

He held his arms out for Jasper, and Mia handed the baby over. He was so small and fragile in Typhoon's arms, and that sense of not knowing what he was doing welled up in him again, but with it rose a warmth in his chest and a surging feeling of love and protectiveness. Whatever the future held, he'd be there with his mate and child, keeping them safe and holding them close, no matter what it took.

He smiled up at Mia. “I love you.”

Mia leaned forward and brushed her mouth against his. “And I love you.”

He caught her hand, pressed a kiss to it, and started to work his way up the inside of her arm.

Mia let out a shivering sigh, and she tangled her fingers into his hair with her free hand.

“Jasper just went to sleep. We should have at least an hour if we put him down carefully.”

It took Typhoon half a second to understand what she meant. In the next half second, he was on his feet and tugging her inside. Mia laughed as they transferred Jasper gently to her arms.

She told him where the bedroom was and disappeared into the nursery to put the baby down.

Typhoon admired the large bed in her room before he undid his shirt.

Just as he tugged it off, he heard a tut-tut behind him and turned to find Mia standing there with her hands on her hips and a sparkle in her eyes.

“Didn't you think I'd want to see that?”

Typhoon arched a brow and then grinned at her. He turned and pulled the garment off entirely before dropping it to the floor. He started on his pants, keeping his movements languid.

Mia watched, her lip clenched between her teeth. Her eyes darkened in lust, and he felt himself tightening. His gaze ran down her clothed body. Even though she was dressed perfectly modestly, her curves were so enticing that he salivated at the thought of getting a taste of her.

He dropped his pants, kicked off his socks, put his hands on hips, and arched a brow at her. “Your turn.”

“Hmm...I agree.” She sauntered over to him—her hips swaying—and lowered herself to her knees before him. He knew exactly what she was about to do, and a moan of anticipation echoed from his throat. She took him in her hands, stroked him a few times, put the tip of him in her mouth, and everything tightened further.

Typhoon wrapped his hands in her hair, quickly taking account of her rhythm and mimicking it as Mia slurped at him, greedy noises of pleasure coming from her throat. His eyes slid shut as shivers of pleasure ran down the length of him and moved up his spine. She was good, using her tongue on the small cleft in him, then pulling him in as deep as she could take him. Her hot, wet mouth made him growl, leaving him wanting so much more.

Mia pulled back slightly, sitting on her heels as she stroked him with her hand. She smiled up at him, then pulled him back into her mouth. She sucked hard, and such zings of pleasure went through him that he had to pull back to stop from cumming prematurely in her mouth. He clenched his hands and panted before pulling her to her feet.

"Take your clothes off," he ordered roughly. "I'm going to eat your clit until you scream my name."

Mia's eyes sparkled as she removed her clothing, keeping her movements so slow that Typhoon almost did the job for her. She was standing naked before him soon enough. Her thick, sweet scent of arousal curled into his nose, and Typhoon seized her around the waist and tossed her back on the bed. Her breasts bounced as she landed. When he parted her legs and knelt between them, he could already see her glistening with natural lubricant.

She tasted just as good as he remembered. His tongue roamed over her, enjoying her taste before he focused in on her clit. She was already so ready, her clit swollen, her hips bucking under his administration, that he thought she must have been playing with herself while she was sucking him off. Soon enough, she was trembling under him, and he focused his ministrations as her hands wound through his hair.

"Robby," she moaned. He liked the sound of his name on her lips.

Her legs tremble on either side of his ears, and Typhoon eased back, wincing a little as she tugged on his hair before he slid a hand between her legs to take the place of his mouth. He gazed up at her body, naked and bared to him, and a surge of greed and need welled in him. He fought with himself but ultimately gave in with a small snarl, and kissed her up one thigh and over her stomach. He lingered, first at one breast, and then the other, bringing her hard nipples to a full salute. Mia's body arched to him, a cry tearing from her throat when he pushed two fingers inside of her. He curved them and stroked her inside.

Mia's hands reached for him, pulling him down over her with such desperation, his own need was driven even harder.

Typhoon continued to suck on her breast until he tasted milk. He worked his way up her chest and lingered on her neck while she writhed beneath him before he finally claimed her mouth.

"Robby," she gasped against his tongue. "I need you. I want you. Please—"

He stroked her hair away from her face and rested his forehead against hers. She was already clamping down on his fingers, and he slowly removed them. He gave himself few more strokes to make sure he was hard enough and then guided himself into her.

His entrance was smooth, and she shuddered when he found his seat deep inside her. Her eyes slid to half-mast, and her hands slid all over his body. He loved the feel of her fingers on his skin: light, smooth, and loving.

Typhoon stared down into her eyes as he started to move. He kept his strokes deep and even, loving the way Mia's face and neck had turned red. She held onto him, small cries coming from her throat. When she pressed herself to her elbows and nibbled at his neck, something even more powerful started in him. A ball of warmth swelled in his chest, and his loins tightened even more. He concentrated on her, the smell and feel of her as he fought his arousal, desperate to give her everything she deserved.

“Robby,” she moaned once more, and then her back arched.

Her eyes rolled to the back of her head, and she let out a cry. She clamped down on him, squeezing so tightly, stars burst behind his eyes. He dropped his mouth to hers, swallowing her cries as he felt himself empty into her. He thrust harder, wanting it to last longer and harder. She dug her fingers into his back, and her hips bucked wildly.

When they had both finished, they lay there wrapped in each other’s arms. Typhoon nuzzled her neck and shoulders, loving the smell of her. He kissed her gently, again and again.

Maybe he'd once thought that love made you weak, but he knew differently now.

"I love you," he whispered. "Mia Efron, you are my mate."

"Yes, I am." Her fingers wound into his hair. "And you are mine."

Typhoon smiled up at her. "Yeah, I'm yours—soul, heart, and body. You'd better take good care of me."

Mia laughed as she ran her fingers down his back. "I plan to. Don't you worry about that."

*****

THE END

10852254R00150

Printed in Great Britain
by Amazon